Myself and Other Strangers

Maureen Oxley

Myself and Other Strangers

Olympia Publishers
London

www.olympiapublishers.com
OLYMPIA PAPERBACK EDITION

A CIP catalogue record for this title is
available from the British Library.

ISBN: 978-1-84897-802-7

First Published in 2016

Olympia Publishers
60 Cannon Street
London
EC4N 6NP

Printed in Great Britain

Dedications

For my Mum and Dad
who gave me so much
when they had so little.

Acknowledgements

Special thanks to Jack Vettriano
For his inspiration and generosity.

Thank you, too, to my husband John,
my family, friends and fellow writers for believing in me.

Contents

An Imperfect Past

The box smelt the same, even after all these years. The stink of a million sins wrapped up in the sweat of reluctant confessors. There, not for the grace of God and his certain forgiveness, but at the direction of Mother Church. Old habits died hard. Frank felt instinctively for the list screwed up in his pocket, along with his lucky marble, the hairy gob-stopper and the pen-knife – but the smooth silk lining yielded no such childish comforts, only a reminder of how far he had come since the days when he had feared the terrors of hell for missing his evening prayers.

He peered into the grille and a dark shadow peered back; a disembodied head still separated from its shoulders, still bobbing about in the unrelenting blackness, still waiting. Only a whiff of cigarette smoke and stale Guinness identified its owner as vaguely human.

"Bless me Father, for I have sinned. It's thirty-two years since my last confession, and these are my sins."

The mantra came easily. Frank remembered how he'd practised on his dad for weeks on end before his 'First Confession'. He'd dressed him up in a black coat and tied a strip of old white sheeting round his neck. It had all been very realistic. His Dad had even given him penance, usually two 'Our Fathers' and three 'Hail Marys' and three nights of washing up for his mother.

"And so ... What are your sins?" Now that Frank's eyes were accustomed to the darkness, he could see that the head had eyes and that they were squinting wearily at the prospect of a listing of the transgressions of more than three decades.

"Well, it's just the one, really. I've killed somebody."

It was hard to know where to start. Father Burns's encouragement to "Start at the beginning" was no help whatsoever – because Frank didn't know where the beginning was. He only knew about the end: the phone call; the hospital; the end. He supposed he'd better start with that.

"She swallowed a hundred paracetamol, Father."

"And did you make her?"

"Yes."

"You opened her mouth and forced them down her throat?"

Frank put his head in his hands. This was going to be difficult. How could he explain about the cine films he'd dug out of the loft? The family history. *His* family history – condensed into ten reels of celluloid. She'd been so excited. He remembered how he'd laughed when he'd opened the door and seen her, all 'dolled up' like she was going somewhere really special.

"What's with the evening dress and the stilettos?" he'd asked, pulling her into his arms. "We're only gonna watch a few home movies."

She'd gasped in mock horror and draped herself provocatively on the chair next to the projector.

"Home movies, Frank, are worth getting dressed up for. We didn't have home movies in our house, I can tell you. Just a few snaps in an old biscuit tin."

They'd sat there all evening. The years had rolled by in the smoky haze of Benson and Hedges and forgotten memories. She'd 'ooh-ed' and 'aah-d' and chortled from time to time. He'd stood silently, enjoying Proustian moments and giving an occasional clout to the old projector. His fifth birthday. Best forgotten but now showing at a cinema near you. He'd smelt again the chocolate train-shaped birthday cake but the home baking hadn't masked the stink of piss on the carpet ... or the whisky ... or the vomit. Nor had the familiar rendition of '*Happy Birthday to You*' drowned out the foulness of his father's temper.

She'd turned to him and smiled.

"You were so lucky. We couldn't afford birthday parties."

Lucky. The word didn't fit into his past. She'd been the lucky one. They'd grown up together in the same street; gone to the same primary school – but that was where the similarity had ended. He used to see her in the park with her mum and dad, sandwiches and bottles of pop spread out on a tartan rug.

"Only spam! Nothing posh" she'd said when he'd told her, years later, how much he'd envied her. He'd have given anything for spam and a bottle of Vimto and the laughter and the fun; he'd have gladly swapped his holidays in the Lake District for even one game of football with his dad on the back lawn that his mother manicured every Sunday afternoon while his father was in the pub. His mum had been good at keeping up appearances. He'd had two mums. The one who screamed and cussed as she took the nightly beatings and the other who made Victoria sponge for the church fete and collected for lepers. His Dad didn't go to church. He hadn't set foot in St Monica's since Father Murphy had hit him round the head with a brass candlestick when he was a lad - and all because he'd dropped the sacred host, the body of Christ. Frank remembered how he'd thought this story very strange – Christ had been nailed to a cross and spat at and his body was in tatters, but he'd forgiven his attackers. Surely he would have been able to forgive a little lad who'd dropped him accidentally.

The church had been a strange place to Frank. Frightening and confusing. He hadn't been able to understand why he had to be a 'God-fearing Christian', why he had to be afraid of someone who was loving and caring.

Although it was still beyond his understanding, he did fear God. That's why he was here, today, adding his contribution to the stink and sweat and his sin to the fuel of burning hell.

The thought of burning hell brought Frank back to Father Burns. He stared intently at the grille and answered the priest's last question.

"No, I didn't make her swallow the tablets, Father, but it was my fault that she did."

The bobbing head moved forward and changed its shape like

some amorphous alien and as it did, it emitted a deep and exasperated sigh that wafted through the confessional. Frank closed his eyes again and held his breath so that he didn't breathe in the stench of the sweat and the sin. He couldn't believe it still made his stomach churn and his heart pound with fear.

Father Burns was getting rather tired of this. He had to break all the rules of a confessor and ask a direct question.

"Why did she swallow the tablets, man?"

His voice rasped with irritation and a desire to get this over and done with as soon as possible.

"Get on with it, man!"

Hurrying, fumbling for words, Frank explained how she'd gasped when she'd seen the pictures of his First Holy Communion Day. The little brides of Christ in their white veils and frothy dresses and the lovely lads in red sashes with crooked grins. In the centre of the scene sat the Parish Priest who'd prepared and nurtured them for this momentous day.

Frank had laughed when he saw her surprise. In fact, he hadn't laughed, he'd chortled merrily as he'd recalled the details of the rite of passage that was the focus of the picture.

"Bet you can't remember the answers to the Catholic Catechism questions," he challenged her. "We learned them off by heart and God help us if we got one word wrong! Try this one:

Who made the world?

She'd answered immediately, her voice as distant as the memory.

God made the world.

Where is God?

God is everywhere

Her voice had dropped to a whisper

Does God See Us?

God sees us and watches over us.

Frank had the feeling that something was wrong. She was barely audible and her face was whiter than pale. She continued the response:

God knows all things, even our most secret thoughts, words and actions.

She stood up and walked towards him, arms outstretched. Frank was beginning to feel afraid. This wasn't her. She was someone else in her body. She repeated the response but this time there were extra words which were totally unfamiliar to him.

God knows all things, even our most secret thoughts and actions ... but God wants us to keep these things secret and if we breathe a word of them to anyone we will burn in hell.

Frank held her in his arms and tried to comfort her as she'd poured out the memories of the evenings in the sacristy when she'd had the honour of polishing the chalice and the candlesticks because she was such a good girl. But he couldn't quell the sobs and the heaving and she'd vomited a million sins and drenched him in the stinking sweat of a soul possessed.

Father Burns listened.

"It wasn't your fault ..."

The voice was softer now and the bobbing head was stilled. It watched Frank as he sobbed and it felt the sweat run down its own neck and bounce off the collar which attached it to his scrawny neck. It smelt the shit of fear as the memory bounced around. Father Burns shook his head but he could not make the pictures disappear. He saw the girl's lips, red and pouting, as she licked her lips, savouring the communion wine she'd downed in one. He hadn't been able to stop her. "It's just like a proper date!" she'd gurgled as she'd pressed herself into him, rubbing her chest into his until he could feel the hardness of her nipples; pressing her body into his groin like some inebriated hoola dancer until his penis did not know itself. He heard her giggling – louder, louder, louder – as he pulled up her skirt and let his fingers savour the delights of Eve's juice which he had never felt before. He felt the softness of her thighs and, even though his eyes were tightly shut, he saw her tongue dart out, snake-like, as she leaned towards him, still giggling: "Kiss me father, for I have sinned. It is two weeks since my last confession and these are my sins." And then he took her, sins and all, and did what he had to do. She'd touched his heart, then squeezed it and wrenched it from its cage of ribs and human frailty. And now he knew for certain, as he had preached a thousand times: God is everywhere and God sees us and watches over us and God knows all things, even our most secret thoughts, words and actions.

Father Burns stared out from the grille and a dark shadow peered back; a disembodied head separated from its shoulders. The face of conscience.

Frank listened to the silence and to the whiff of cigarette smoke and the stale Guinness and waited. The old man was dressed up in a black coat with a strip of old white sheeting tied around his neck.

"And have you anything else to confess?"

"No, Father. Nothing of substance."

"Then say your *Act of Contrition* and I'll absolve you from your sins."

The words did not come easily after all these years. Frank stuttered and stammered his Act of Contrition:

"O my God, I am heartily sorry for having offended Thee ..."

He was suddenly aware that his was not the only voice in the stinking box. The rasping words of Father Burns added a depth to his prayer – a three-dimensional acclamation that made the hairs on the back of Frank's neck stand on end:

"....and I detest all my sins, because I dread the loss of Heaven, and the pains of Hell..."

The two men fell silent and a shaft of sunlight lit the confessional, illuminating the dark shadow behind the grille and giving a more human form to the disembodied head.

Frank waited for his penance. He was not disappointed.

"Say two 'Our Fathers' and three 'Hail Marys'"

"Thank you, Father."

Frank got up, anxious to leave the darkness and get out into the sunshine.

Baby, Bye Bye

Night after night, she dreamt of what might have been. She'd stir from a troubled sleep in the hotness of middle-age and almost hear his gravelly voice vomiting split infinitives and laughing when she squirmed at his protestations that he **would of** been on time if the traffic hadn't been so heavy. That same voice was as smooth as velvet when they lay alone. He'd whisper in her ear and, in his lilting Dublin accent, softly sing love songs which betrayed no sign at all of his mission to massacre the English language. Then, fully awake, she'd almost feel the gentle touch of his rough hands on her skin.

It was on such a night that the laughter and the voices seemed louder and more real than usual. Marianne opened the window to get some air and then lay on the bed which mocked her. Her silk nightdress was stuck to her – the result of a conspiracy between a sultry August night and burning desire. If Tom were here, he'd laugh. He'd throw back his head and guffaw with that deep-throated roar that's fuelled by undiluted testosterone:

"Take it off, you silly cow. I don't know why you wear it. Anybody'd think you didn't want me to see you in the buff ..."

Then he'd grab her and try to pull the straps down. She'd pretend to struggle ... but only for a short while, until she could wait no longer. And then she'd step out of the damp blackness and lie on the cool, white sheets – spread-eagled: waiting for his examination. That was her little fantasy. It made him laugh. He'd run his hands all over her body, a bit at a time, announcing his diagnoses as he did so:

"Lovely legs, Mrs. Davidson ... Now open wide ... ...no problems there, either! And as for these lovely tits ... ... never seen a better pair in all my life......"

And when, finally, the examination was over, she'd say: "Are you ready to give me the injection now, Doctor" and he'd laugh again.

"You love it don't you, Mrs Davidson? It keeps you young, doesn't it?" and he'd give her a mighty slap on the bottom and she'd say, "Careful, that hurts!" and he'd tell her that was what happened if you let yourself get examined by a brickie.

She smiled as she remembered how people had scowled when she'd married Tom. It was hard to tell who'd scowled most- her friends and relations or his. She recalled her sister's horrified expression as she curled her lip:

"For God's sake, Marianne. Having a bit of rough on the side is one thing, but marrying him! It doesn't bear thinking about! Think about the implications for your career, for heaven's sake! Who wants to be represented in court by a barrister married to a bricklayer?"

Marianne had pointed out that it was just possible that her clients were more concerned about her ability to articulate an argument than about her taste in men. She'd also reminded her sister that her first husband, for all his professional acumen, had not acquitted himself well in their marriage, mainly because he had little interest in life outside the stock exchange.

In spite of their apparent incompatibility, life had been good for a while. Tom kept Marianne's feet on the ground and she helped him to hold his head up high. She gave him back the confidence and self-respect that was stolen from him by the cruelty of a loveless childhood. Through her relationship with Tom, she was able to nurture an empathy with human need and a passionate desire for social justice. She had not been inured to such qualities in her own privileged upbringing. Marianne was the richer for being Tom's wife and he, in turn, benefited in no small way from the material wealth and comfort which her work provided.

It had been this mutual need which had bound them together through the ups and downs of their years together. The arrival of their beautiful daughter strengthened those bonds.

Marianne sighed deeply as she recalled the ultimate challenge which had tested their marriage. She'd known when she married him that he had 'an eye for the ladies' – and, indeed, they were attracted to him like wasps to a jam jar. They laughed at his jokes, fluttered their eyelashes and generally flirted with the utmost blatancy, whether or not Marianne was there. They just couldn't help themselves. And he, in turn, received their flirtations as though they were the first he'd ever encountered. Once, at a party, Marianne had told a friend that to watch Tom doing what he did best was like watching Adam and Eve discovering their sexuality for the first time. The rejoinder had been cynical and hurtful:

"Or like watching an un-neutered tom cat sniffing about ...... he's got the right name any way!"

"That's out of order! Tom just appreciates women."

"Doesn't it worry you? If he behaves like this when you're around, what do you think he does when you're not?"

Marianne had been furious. She trusted Tom implicitly and she strongly resented any implication that he'd ever be unfaithful. That was why it had been such a shattering blow when she found out about the affair. He'd been distraught when she confronted him with it – told her that the girl had thrown herself at him; given it to him on a plate. What was a man to do? As hurt as she was, she'd believed him. Hadn't she watched the way women behaved around him? How was he supposed to react? He was a red-blooded male, after all. She could vouch for that. So she'd forgiven him and they'd put the whole matter behind them. Got on with their lives. She'd never mentioned it again. That was part of the deal. She'd never mention it again. He'd never do it again.

"I'm learning a lot from you, Marianne. I plead guilty and get a reduced sentence!"

He'd howled raucously, oblivious of the hurt on his wife's face – hurt which quickly turned to anger and inspired a lengthy rhetoric worthy of any court in the land.

"The 'reduced sentence', as you so succinctly put it, is more for my benefit than yours. I have no wish ever to mention it gain. I have no wish to relive the sordid incident. I have no wish for anyone to find out that you keep your brains in your trousers. I have no wish for my friends and family to have the satisfaction of saying 'I told you so'. I have no wish to remind myself that you're a low-life scum bag with the morals of an alley cat. That, Tom, is why you have a 'reduced sentence'. We could more rightfully call it a 'suspended sentence' – because if you are ever unfaithful again, not only will I mention it again, I will hang you from the banister by your balls until you scream for mercy. Do I make myself clear?"

The next few years had passed by quite uneventfully and Marianne assumed that she had indeed made herself quite clear. Even the flirting had been toned down. Tom obviously had no intention of incurring her wrath and testing the sincerity of her threats. She'd been glad she'd given him another chance. She'd assumed he'd learned his lesson. There had been nothing to suggest that he had as much as looked at another women since his first offence. Nothing, that is, until she found the credit card statement and made some discreet enquiries of the Kings Head Hotel in Borrington regarding the reservation of 10 July when he was supposed to be at a stag night in Dublin. Then she'd used some useful contacts to establish the identity of his bed mate – one 'Tracey Goddard', local tart and barmaid.

She'd decided not to challenge him for several days. She couldn't bear to hear the pathetic excuses. She already had a good idea of a string of possible excuses for his defence. It was an occupational hazard. She really didn't want to hear that he'd booked a double room in Borrington to 'surprise her' but that he'd decided against it at the last minute; or that someone had stolen his credit card. She didn't want to hear it.

But the days had become weeks and then months and Marianne had to face the realisation that she didn't want to challenge him at all. Not then. Not ever. She recalled her vitriolic threats after his last little fling. He'd known that he had nothing to lose. She'd made an empty threat – she could never face the humiliation of telling a single soul. She knew that it would be she who would be the loser if she confronted him. She'd known that he'd leave – and everyone would say "Well – what did you expect?"

She couldn't bear the idea. Nor could she entertain the prospect of nights alone. She needed him more than he now needed her and so did their daughter who idolised her father. She couldn't let him go. She decided to reserve her right to remain silent – and she'd known that in making this decision she was bound to a lifetime of silence. She'd understood that there would be affairs for the rest of their married life. She'd come to terms with that. She could just about live with it. Their marriage had withstood the ultimate challenge.

It had been a long hot day. The traffic had been at a standstill, as usual. They'd edged forward slowly, cursing the hold-up. The airport was still more than five miles away! Thoughts of whether they'd be there in time for the flight had been interrupted by the unmistakable sound of metal on metal. Glancing in the mirror, she saw the red Renault which had embedded itself in the boot. A young man was getting out and Marianne threw open the door of the car and shouted:

"You're a bloody imbecile. That's what you are. A bloody imbecile. You shouldn't be allowed to drive a car! You're not safe."

She'd said it in frustration and temper. How could she have known that the boy had mental health problems; that he was in the care of the community; that he wasn't taking his drugs. He opened the door and grabbed Marianne by her collar. Tom grabbed the boy to pull him off. And he beat Tom around the head with the crow bar he kept under the seat to protect himself from the enemies who shouted in his head.

They'd said that Tom could be in the coma for days or weeks; that if he came out of it, they had no idea what state he'd be in. She wondered if he'd be brain damaged.

They'd played music to him – John Lennon, mostly. Imagine. Imagine life without him. Imagine life with him. What was the lesser of the two evils?

Marianne pulled up on the car park and prepared herself for another visit. If only he would speak, she wouldn't care what the words were. Funny how perspectives change.

"Mummy! Mummy"

She spotted their daughter running towards her across the car park. Her heart lurched – she probably had news; maybe he'd responded to the music. Perhaps he'd opened his eyes. But the news had been bad. Marianne had listened as Sonia had sobbed the details of his continuing coma.

"We've got to prepare ourselves! Daddy's not going to get better!"

"We're not going to give up," Marianne murmured. "We must have hope."

Hope was what had taken her to the seedy pub, searching for Tracey. She'd found her sitting at the bar, eyeing up the talent, looking for a meal ticket. She'd cringed as she'd approached her, but Tracey had been more surprised than her, especially when she told her what she wanted.

"Just talk to him," she'd begged.

"What about?"

About...you know ..."

Marianne had coloured up and looked down before taking a step forward and looking Tracey straight in the eye. Tracey had stared back, her open mouth and panda eyes confirming the older woman's perceptions.

"No, I don't know. I don't know what the bloody 'ell yer on about. You want me to talk to a bloke who can't hear me about a dirty weekend that ended in a bust up?"

Marianne had got brave and moved even closer, grabbing the girl's arm.

"I want you to try to save him. I want him to hear your voice. I want him to smell that revolting cheap scent that you wear. I want him to open his eyes and see the trowelled on make-up and the plunging cleavage. I want you to wake him up.

"I can't. It's spooky"

"You can. You owe him that much."

Marianne had clenched her teeth in frustration and turned away. Tracey followed her.

There had been no twitching finger or barely perceptible breath. No sign of life. No gradual awakening. He'd just opened his eyes and stared at Tracey.

"Ow yer doin' Tom?"

Tom looked blank. He said nothing.

"See! He doesn't want to speak to me, I told you we had a bust up!"

And Tracey, her debt paid, had sauntered out of their lives.

Each day, Tom got stronger, his waking days longer but silent. He wasn't going to walk again, let alone lay bricks. Life was going to be very hard. Very different. Almost too hard for Marianne to bear.

She considered the options. She re-considered them. She thought of little else, day or night – and this night was no exception.

She got off the bed and slipped on her white silk negligee. She looked at herself in the full length mirror. She sighed, remembering, and stroked her breasts until her nipples stood proud. The window slammed open and the curtain billowed in an unexpected wind. A changing wind. Still naked, she moved to close the window.

Tom reached out from beneath the cool white sheets and touched her.

Dance Me to the End of Love

Your head nods slowly in time to the unheard music. A hint of a smile touches your lips. I ask you what you see; what you hear. The smile gets broader and you touch my face, stroking my cheeks and my lips.

"I see you, my darling. It's our wedding day..." Your voice is strong – stronger than any part of your body.

"I love the dress – the diamante butterfly on the back. It's so you!"

I'm startled at the words. I gasp. How can a man whose body is so wrecked possess a mind that can remember my wedding dress in such detail? Everyone's wedding's special but ours had been so very special. It had been 1951 and you were only 24 years old – the same age as me.

"I still have the dress ..."

I lean forward and brush my cheek against yours and it's 1951 again and my heart is racing with the passion of it all. But now your skin is leathery and cold and the fingers that grip mine are all but dead. I rest my head on your chest and I can hear your heart beating strongly. I fancy it's in time to the music. I wonder which song is in your head. Maybe our special song. I mouth the words – silently.

'Dance me to the wedding now ...'

Your voice booms back.

"You still have the dress? Well, you still have the body, my darling."

And you reach out and twist my hair into a knot around your fingers and we embrace in a silent duet.

"I love making babies with you. Let's do it all again."

I talk to you for a while about our babies – about our beautiful daughter, our only child. Our song is till bouncing around my head:

'Dance me to the children who are asking to be born ...'

I take you back to 1955 and remind you of her third birthday. We had a little party – just for the family. I made a jelly in a rabbit-shaped mould and she cried when you ate its ears and told her you'd eat hers next! You picked her up and twirled her round, singing as you went:

On the farm, every Friday
On the farm, it's rabbit pie day.
So, every Friday that ever comes along,
I get up early and sing this little song
Run rabbit - run rabbit - Run! Run! Run!
Run rabbit - run rabbit - Run! Run! Run!

She cried until she laughed and I laughed until I cried as you held her on one arm and me in the other, binding us together in a family dance that went on forever.

You chuckle at the memory now and stroke my neck. I tremble with delight. You laugh softly.

"You were cross that I'd upset her. That's why you were crying. 'For God's sake,' you said, after we'd put her to bed; 'give the bloody war songs a rest. The war's been over for sixteen years.'

I shudder. We didn't have many rows but we always enjoyed making up didn't we? Making love was so special. I remember the first time. The classy hotel on the Devon Riviera. Such opulence! A million miles away from the little terraced houses that were our family homes. A sumptuous fish dinner and a bottle of Chateauneuf-du-Pape followed by dancing to the Frank Zelder Band. Then up to bed to a late dessert of tender loving laced with coyness and wary exploration. I bet you can't remember the dress I wore on that night!

You close your eyes, still smiling and I ask you what you are thinking about?

****

He closes his eyes and smiles, remembering their first time. Mrs Fogarty's boarding house in Torquay. The best they could afford.

He can still remember the blue of her dress and her sun kissed hair. They'd shared a meal of fish and chips and a bottle of cheap red wine in a sea-front cafe and then danced all the way back to their digs ... back to their room, giggling and expectant. They hadn't been disappointed as they clung together in their first lesson in love. They'd explored each other's bodies with naivety tenderness and moved onwards towards the passion of it all.

When the sun came up, they became two again, rolling apart and dropping off the bed onto the threadbare carpet. Seeing her beautiful body in the sobriety of daylight, he'd suddenly felt shy and turned his back and looked for his clothes. Her blue dress lay next to his trousers, crumpled and stained with red wine. He'd dressed hurriedly and sat on the edge of the bed, stroking her neck and contemplating for the first time the crumples and stains of the other business of life which would be a part of their marriage and which they would face together. She'd opened her eyes and they'd embraced tenderly, wrapped up in the wonderful realization of pure love. They understood the completeness of it all and it had sustained them throughout their days together, as their family had grown.

****

You startle me with another flash of lucidity. "*Our baby .... she has babies of their own – and they're growing up, too. Our grandchildren are nearly the same age now as we were when we first met.*" Your memory is sharp and alert.

I squeeze your hand. "That's a wonderful age to be."

The smile disappears and your jaw tightens. I ask you if you are in pain. You close your eyes. Your breathing is laboured and beads of perspiration stand out on your forehead.

****

He closes his eyes. His breathing is laboured and beads of perspiration stand out on his forehead. It's 1944 and a cold crisp autumn. The furnaces work overtime as the inmates are dispatched as speedily as possible. A fog of smoke and ash hangs over the barbed wire and slime, anonymising the environment as much as its inhabitants. They are lost in the fog – disorientated. The cattle trucks have ejected them at the ungodly terminus. Whole families have been torn limb from limb; their hair, clothing and personal belongings ripped from them in a well-rehearsed act of depersonalisation. It takes only two and a half minutes to steal an identity. It takes just a little longer for many, so traumatized, to forget their own name. But those who can remember anything can just about identify the religious holidays which for so long have demarcated the year along with the signposts of the seasons. He is among those who have been 'selected' for a shower. He knows the truth of it. It's late enough in history to know the truth. Gas will cleanse their bodies and purge their souls and the shower will remain dry except for the tears of the just.

****

Your breathing is rapid. Your chest rises and falls with panic and anguish. I pray that your mind is still and that the gasps of fear are not a desperate articulation of the terror of the past which I'd hoped you'd buried in the fullness of your life.

****

He grimaces at the terror of it all. It's 1944. It's the holiday of Simchat Torah – a day for rejoicing. He's standing up in the bathhouse and shouting: "We have nothing – but let's celebrate for one last time before we die. We have no clothes, no names, no torah; we have no music; we have no wives or sisters, no brothers or children with whom to dance. So let's dance with God before we give him back what belongs to him."

He sings with his comrades, softly: "*Ashreinu mah tov chelkeinu u'mah nayim goraleinu umah yafah yerushateinu...*" (How fortunate are we and how wonderful is our portion and how beautiful is our heritage.) But such defiance does not please the Nazi guard who hears the revelry. He has heard a hundred times or more the weeping, the sobbing, the recitations and incantations of the nearly-dead and it hasn't touched his heart. But this is different. He will not have singing and dancing in the showers. It is unthinkable. He asks you why you are doing this. He tells the guard, boldly and insolently:

"We're rejoicing at leaving the beasts behind and meeting our families again. We rejoice at the thought of facing our God who knows us all by name not number and who will restore our failing bodies and our wounded souls."

****

You are fighting as you fought then. But now the fight is easier. There is no sadist who pulls you away from the jaws of death because it is too good for you; there is no Nazi officer to drag this singing boy by his neck to a place of torture to repay him for his rebellion. But you know there is a God ... for God sends you help in the form of a high ranking officer who has travelled from Berlin to round up slave labour for work camps. He is looking for young, able-bodied men who are fit enough to work hard in appalling conditions. As this man strides through the camp he sees you and your fellow rebels. You are all still high on the opium of unexpected reprieve and not yet cowed by the plans of your captor. You still radiate strength and vitality.

"Excellent," the Nazi officer smiles in satisfaction. "Exactly the type of boys I need."

And you leave the camp as you entered ... in the back of a cattle truck. But this time you are singing to the hollow notes of the camp orchestra. The scraping of the fiddles accompanies no screams of joy and fervour or stamping feet – only guilt and self-reproach.

Your voice breaks into my thoughts. Perfectly in tune; strong in its frailty.

"Dance me to your beauty with a burning violin
Dance me through the panic till I'm safely gathered in""

I gasp. So, that song *is* in your head, just as it's in mine. They played it at our granddaughter's wedding and it became 'our song'. Our children cringed at the idea of their mother and father singing contemporary love songs.

But the dance isn't over yet. I hold you close and clasp your hands, our fingers intertwining. I whisper softly: "You have your clothes, a name, a torah; we have music; you have a wife with whom to dance. So let's dance with God before we give him back what belongs to him."

My trembling voice lifts us above the pathos of the moment.

Dance me to the end of love. Dance me to the end of love

Your story ends in the stillness of the now:

Ashreinu mah tov chelkeinu u'mah nayim goraleinu umah yafah yerushateinu.

And then the music stops.

Dressed to Kill

"Are you Roger John Phillips?"

The deep blue eyes of Owen Dryband looked accusingly over the top of his spectacles and Roger John Phillips shuffled his feet, wishing that he were not. He nodded unconvincingly.

"Then I am instructed, Mr Phillips, to give you this letter. As you will see, it is from your former wife, Catherine Mary Phillips."

The current Mrs. Phillips stood stiffly by her husband's side. At the mention of Catherine's name, she arched her back, extended her fingers so that they joined at the tips and tilted back her head enquiringly. Mrs. Susan Phillips was not happy.

The sound of Catherine's name had taken Susan back to the first time she'd ever seen her. She'd called into the office one morning and Susan, Roger's ever-efficient secretary, had made her a coffee while she waited for her husband. She'd been taller than Susan had imagined. She'd always thought that they'd look alike – but she couldn't have been more wrong. From the top of her curly-permed head to the tip of her sensible shoes, Catherine Mary Phillips was everything that Susan had strived not to be. She was the girl in the corner of the playground the others told her to ignore. She was the girl next door doing tomorrow's homework instead of going to the disco – the one they called a 'stuck-up cow'. She was boredom personified and yet, in spite of all that, they'd become the best of friends. They'd met each Tuesday for lunch and often took a stroll along the river putting the world to rights. As different as chalk and cheese.

Susan and Catherine had, however, had quite a lot in common. Roger John Phillips. Lecher and adulterer of this parish. As smooth and slippery as the soles on his expensive Italian shoes. A man with an eye for a presentable woman with a healthy bank balance. He'd been happy enough with Catherine until Susan had appeared on the scene. It had been the old, old story ......

But Susan had reined him in. Like an aging tom-cat, he'd marked out his territory with all the conventions of monogamous domesticity. He'd got the cream! Eight hundred grand from Catherine in the divorce settlement and the exclusive rights to the best sex in London from his gorgeous new wife.

Mr Dryband coughed disapprovingly, as though he had been privy to Roger's scandalous behaviour and had some sort of opinion on the matter. In fact, he was merely wondering how much longer it was going to be before the business in hand was concluded. He glanced at the clock. He had another appointment at 10.30 am. Meanwhile Roger wracked his brains wondering what this was all about. It occurred to him that Catherine had been bad-mouthing him again. Probably looking for more maintenance. Moaning about the cost of living. She was good at that, but she usually harangued him over the phone. This lot was a bit dramatic. Dragging them both down to her solicitors and putting it in writing.

The handwriting was as beautiful as ever – it was the only really attractive thing about her. She always used a fountain pen. Roger smiled wryly as he tore open the envelope. She was still so old-fashioned. The immaculately scribed words taunted him, even before he read them. So precise. Sitting neatly on the line. He could almost see her taking the folded blotting paper out of her stationery box. How many people used blotting paper these days, for God's sake? Or a stationery box, for that matter.

He supposed she still cooked beef casserole every Wednesday and fish pie on a Friday – such a creature of habit that she had the best-trained bowels in Islington. And then he stopped smiling ... and thinking ... and supposing – as the words jumped off the page and flung themselves into his consciousness, bringing him back to the present.

Mr Dryband glanced at the clock again, less discreetly on this occasion, and cleared his throat. It had taken Roger exactly eight minutes to read the letter and digest its contents. That was about two minutes longer than it had taken him to tell Catherine that he was leaving her for another woman – for Susan. Roger's stomach churned as he remembered the coolness of her reaction. He might have been telling her that he was fed up with beef casserole on a Wednesday; that he fancied something a bit spicier, like chilli con carne. She'd been cleaning the windows at the time. That was why he could remember that it had been the third Monday of the month. She hadn't even turned to look at him. Still working relentlessly on a stubborn smear she'd simply said, "Well, Roger. I can't say I'm happy about it but I do understand. Susan's a very lovely woman. She's everything I'm not."

Part of him had been relieved that she'd taken it so well, but he'd also been more than a little peeved. He was used to women fighting over him. He'd expected at least some indignation. But that had come later – when the settlement was sorted.

Susan raised an eyebrow and peered at her husband's face with some alarm. His face had the cold pallor of a man who'd had a terrible shock. She realised that, whatever news the letter contained, it had been read but certainly not digested. It was stuck in his throat like some ghastly bone from a Friday fish pie.

"Well?"

"She's dead."

Susan's face relaxed a little. Moving towards her husband, she stroked his face. Her pleasure was barely concealed. She wasn't really surprised that Catherine had finally gone. She'd enjoyed ill health for years. It had started with the diabetes the year after Roger had left. And then the high blood pressure and the angina. It had been her own fault. She'd neglected herself. Let herself go. Piled on the pounds. She'd never been blessed with much of a body, but she could have made more effort for goodness sake. You had to try harder as you got older.

"Would you like to sit down, Mrs Phillips?" Mr Dryband pointed to the leather chair beside his desk. Susan sat down, crossed her legs and removed a stray hair from the front of her black coat with its black fur collar. Roger liked her in this coat. He'd persuaded her to wear it today.

"Perfect," he murmured as he kissed her cheek. "Smart but sexy. DTK as always."

DTK was Roger's shorthand for 'Dressed To Kill'. It was his ultimate compliment.

Susan, like Mr Dryband, was getting just a little impatient. She sank back into the leather, running the palms of her hands along the arms of the soft contours of his favourite chair

Mr Dryband's breathing quickened; beads of perspiration appeared on his brow. He moistened his lips and coughed again. But this time the cough was not disapproving as the eyes of Owen Dryband looked over the top of his spectacles at the legs of Susan Phillips. She leaned forward in the chair and as she did so her breasts fell forward and occupied almost all of his field of vision. Cursing his maker for his short-sightedness, he pushed his glasses back into their rightful position and stared hard at the vision of loveliness which sat before him

Susan smiled. She loved her body just as much as men did. That was why she took such good care of it. She didn't care how much she spent. Roger could afford it. Money was no object. Only the best was good enough. Her next project was already planned. A 'nip and tuck' to sort out that bit of sagging skin on her tummy and then another face-lift. Roger didn't like her to talk about it. He always loved the final result but he didn't want to hear about the details. He was a bit squeamish, was Roger, about the cutting and the sutures. He came over all peculiar if anyone talked about their operations – started to tremble and sweat.

Roger was still standing with the letter in his hand. He couldn't believe she'd actually done it! She'd threatened it often enough but they say that the ones who threaten it never do it, so he'd taken no notice. He'd ignored her. Just thought she was trying to upset things between him and Susan. He didn't care about the way that she'd done away with herself. He didn't care about the fact that she blamed him and hoped he'd rot in hell. He didn't care about anything at the moment except that he thought that he was going to throw up. Roger felt squeamish. He'd come over all peculiar. He started to sweat and tremble.

Susan moved across the room with the urgency of a woman who knew about cleaning up vomit. She had no wish to witness another one of Roger's funny little turns in here, thank you very much – or anywhere else for that matter.

"Take deep breaths and pull yourself together!" She spat the words out of the side of her mouth with all the sympathy of a squashed wasp. She'd had enough of this charade. Snatching the letter, she held it arm's length and absorbed the contents, much as one might read a shopping list. Her face was expressionless. She didn't even bat an eyelid when she realised the reason for Catherine's untimely end. Tough! She should have pulled herself together – sorted her head out.

But when she reached the last paragraph, she understood. She knew why Roger was retching and heaving and Mr Dryband's secretary was ushering him from the room. As the words sank in, she pursed her lips and frowned and the feet of a thousand crows landed pitilessly on her face.

I'm not worried about dying, Roger. I've done a great deal of research, as you can imagine, and I've selected the most painless way. There won't be a mark on me. It's just a pity about the post-mortem. That will mess me up a bit. I've researched the procedure in great detail. First of all there will be the external examination. The pathologist will record the appearance of my body, noting any marks, bruises or wounds. Swabbed specimens will be taken, for analysis, from my mouth, breasts, vagina and rectum. Then a

large Y-shaped incision will be made behind each ear and will extend down
the sternum to my groin. The pathologist will peel back my skin, exposing
my neck and chest, revealing the bones, muscles and organs inside my body.
Then my breastbone will be cut through, in order to remove my lungs and
heart. A circular saw will cut round my skull and its top will be prized off.
My brain will be removed for further examination ....

Susan closed her eyes and touched her stomach, as if to reassure it. She stroked her neck with her index finger and traced an invisible line around the contours of her face. She wanted to tell her body that all would be well, but she knew that Roger would now take a great deal more reassuring when he assessed the results of the next round of surgical improvement. She wondered if he'd ever be able to touch her again, or, worse still ...... Susan didn't know what was the more worrying – the prospect of Roger's declining sexual interest or the possibility of his unwillingness to fund her frequent visits to her plastic surgeon. She sighed deeply and, tossing the letter onto Mr Dryband's desk, returned to the comfort of the brown chair. It was an impressive chair – antique leather with a studded back and trimmed with brass studs. She wondered how much it had cost. It smelt expensive and satisfying. It smelt like Mr Dryband.

Mr Dryband coughed, very politely, and Susan wondered whether this persistent complaint was irritating him as much as it was irritating her.

"Mrs Phillips, there's something for you, too. I am instructed to give you this."

Susan eyed the small parcel suspiciously. It looked harmless enough. She took the box and opened it slowly, hesitantly, as one might open a bank statement the week after Christmas. As the content became apparent, a stereophonic gasp broke the tense silence in the solicitor's office. Mr Dryband's mouth dropped open. He had been totally unaware that his client had left a gift of such value – and to the woman who'd stolen her husband. He was deeply perplexed. The workings of the female mind were quite an enigma to him.

The diamond in the heart-shaped pendant sparkled in a setting of white gold. Susan knew enough about jewellery to know that this was the real McCoy – about half a carat, at a conservative estimate. She lifted it from the velvet pad, hands trembling at the excitement of such an unexpected gift. So Catherine had forgiven her after all. They say that true friendship can never die. She held it up to her throat and fiddled with the clasp.

"Would you mind, Mr Dryband? I can't quite manage."

Dryband rushed to help, with rather indecent haste, and was delighted to be of assistance.

"There you are, Mrs Phillips. And may I say that the beauty of the jewellery is matched only by that of the neck on which it sits."

Susan smiled, amused by the pedantic style of his flattery and satisfied that the day was turning out to be so much better than she had expected – in every way. Glowing with pleasure, she picked up the small card which lay in the box, anxious to read its message:

A special gift for you from LifeStones Ltd. A new concept in remembering. A new concept in technology. The diamond in this beautiful piece is made with care from the remains of your loved one by a process which we have perfected. Natural diamonds form over thousands of years in subterranean temperatures and under the unimaginable pressure of the earth's crust. Using special machinery which mimics the natural process of diamond formation by speeding up and controlling the pressure-temperature equation, we are able to transform the ashes of that special person in your life into a lasting memorial.

Susan snatched the pendant from her neck, breaking the chain, and hurled it at the wall. She didn't care. She didn't care about anything at the moment except that she thought that she was going to throw up. Susan felt squeamish. She'd come over all peculiar. She started to sweat and tremble. Tears stung her eyes as she read the personal greeting at the bottom of the card, in Catherine's familiar hand:

Just for you, Susan. I'm beautiful now – and worth more than I ever have been.
Catherine xxx

Game On

It was something she'd never done before.

She opened her laptop, looked at the blank screen and snapped the lid shut again in panic.

She told herself not to be so stupid and opened her laptop again. She hoped that she was opening the door to a new life. A better life.

Trawling through the profiles on *DateTec.com* was like stalking a stag party. A gallery of men paraded across the screen - fat, thin and belly-held-in, young, middle-aged and decrepit; handsome, huggable and hideous, all advertising their wares and their wear-nots. The profiles themselves were just as fascinating. Any woman who wanted a man who kept reptiles in his bedroom or who lived with his mother would find something to suit her requirements. Their screen names often gave a bit of clue about what 'sort' they were. *Silver Fox* drove a Jag and wanted a female companion for occasional skiing holidays in Transylvania; *Blue Phantom* didn't make any bones about wanting a one-night stand to avoid time wasting. And then there was the matter of spelling and grammar which, for Lucy, were vital elements of a good profile. They suggested intelligence even if the content was a bit suspect. Conversely, interesting men who wrote profiles about wanting *sole mates*, liking *coastal seenery* or enjoying *fine dinning* were ruled out without hesitation. Similarly eliminated, were men with ginger hair, beards, spots or eyes set too far apart. It was a difficult process finding someone who fitted the bill and Lucy thought it was an almost impossible task. She regretted wasting her money registering with *DateTec.Com*. She certainly wasn't going to waste any more time. She had too much to do. Dating web-sites and social media were a bit of distraction when you worked from home. Too many opportunities for coffee breaks.

Lucy spent the whole morning dealing with audit reports, chasing invoices and other riveting tasks. She was ready for lunch. She'd have a sandwich after she'd checked her emails. There were only three – one informing her that she could win a prize if she signed up for a store card, one about the gas bill and one from *DatingTec.com*. Confirmation of membership? No. Just a minute.

You have an email from Moonshine. Log into your account to view this message.

Hesitation overcame curiosity and she opened the email. She realized she was holding her breath and that her hands were trembling. As soon as she saw Moonshine's picture, she began to relax. He was a pleasant looking guy with no obvious defects. He was tall and dark, seemed to have all his teeth, and his profile would suggest that he lived alone and had no interest in reptiles. Lucy scrutinized the profile line by line, absorbing every detail. He was 35, worked in a bank, and was divorced. He enjoyed going to the theatre, eating out and travelling. There was something very open about his face. He had an honest, sincere look about him. She guessed he was the sort of guy who helped old ladies across the road and bought *The Big Issue*. He finished his email with a request for her to tell him more about herself. All thoughts of lunch disappeared and her fingers clattered across the keyboard in a frenzy of premature enthusiasm.

Thanks for your email Moonshine. I'm the same age as you – 35 years young. I have my own accountancy business working from home. I'm divorced but feel ready to start dating again. We share the same interests really but I must say it's been a long time since I went to the theatre. 'Love Never Dies' was we saw I think. I sometimes go out for a meal with my sister but it's not often and nothing fancy – just a pub meal. My ex wasn't keen on going out at all. Came home from work, had his tea and drifted off to sleep in front of the TV. How long have you been divorced?

Anyway, must close now.

Best wishes

Kitten21

Within an hour or two, another email dropped into the clutter of Lucy's Inbox. It seemed that Moonshine's divorce had been quite amicable (at least he wasn't a wife beater) He'd been divorced for quite a while.

The emails bounced backwards and forwards for three or four days until one day Lucy put her phone number on the bottom of the email. She fancied a real conversation with a real man.

She wasn't disappointed. Moonshine (aka Michael) was fascinating. He had one of those voices. Liquid chocolate. She imagined it running down her throat and licked her lips.

"We had different ideas about what we wanted out of marriage. She was a bit of a socialite really. Always wanting to go out – dinner parties, concerts. She just didn't like being at home."

They chatted for quite a few evenings. Every call lasted exactly an hour. The first hour was 'free' – part of the package. After an hour you had to pay for your phone calls. He always set the timer for 60 minutes on the oven. When it 'dinged' the conversation stopped abruptly and they'd both laugh as they said their hasty goodbyes.

After a couple of weeks, Michael suggested that they meet up for a meal.

"No pub meals," he said. "A bit of fine dining, maybe? Perhaps you'd like to suggest somewhere"

"Well ... There's a little Italian place just opened opposite the police station ..."

"That sounds good. When can you make it? I'll book a table. What's it called?"

"Err ... Cabo Buono. Don't ask me to spell it." Lucy laughed.

"When?"

"When what?"

"When shall I book for?"

"Oh. Erm. I'm free on Thursday."

"Thursday it is then. What time shall I pick you up?"

"Pick me up?" Lucy stomach churned and her brain retrieved all the safety information she'd read about internet dating.

"Oh thanks, but it's fine. I'll make my own way there. 7 o'clock."

"Great. See you then Lucy"

As Thursday got nearer, Lucy got more and more nervous. What should she wear? Something sophisticated? She picked up her favourite green dress with a cowl neck. No. Too formal. After she'd rejected a beaded pink top with a grey skirt and several other little numbers, she finally settled on a black skirt and matching cornelli lace blouse. It was feminine but understated and she always felt good when she wore it. She made an appointment at the hairdressers – her favourite 'hair up' style, a manicure and a facial. This guy had better be worth it.

The taxi dropped her off at exactly 7.05 – she didn't want to be first and anyway it was a woman's prerogative to make a dramatic entrance. The waiter opened the door and showed her to their table. Michael stood up and took her hand. She thought at first he was going to kiss it but he inclined his head and shook her hand, very gently. He was just as handsome as his profile picture. His blue eyes looked her up and down approvingly as he pulled out her seat.

The menus arrived. The food was good and the conversation flowed as easily as the Pinot. They had such a lot in common. They both enjoyed travelling, gardening, and music from the 70s and 80s. Time flew by as they compared visits to Sorrento, Paris and Vancouver; discussed the best sort of potting compost and shared details of their music collections.

"We'd better make a move. Looks like they're getting ready to shut up shop. They'll think we've rented this table."

Michael grinned and Lucy smiled back. She liked Michael and she hoped he liked her enough to see her again.

"I'll drop you home," he said as he helped her on with her coat. "Taxis are hard to come by at this time of night."

This time she didn't protest. Perhaps it was the Pinot. Perhaps it was a sixth sense that he was a decent man. After all, they'd talked for so long one way or another she felt as though she'd known him all her life.

It had started to rain. He put his arm round her and they ran to a smart looking BMW, giggling as they avoided the puddles.

"You'll have to direct me."

"Oh yes. Of course. Turn right at the lights ....now go straight over the next two roundabouts. Not literally." She giggled again. "I'm not good at giving directions."

"Ahh. A woman who likes to be in the driving seat. Don't worry. All roads lead to home"

He turned his head and gave her that cheeky grin again.

"Number 12," She said. "There. The one with the mini on the drive"

He stopped the car and turned off the engine.

"Am I being too forward or do you trust me enough to ask me in for a coffee?

Lucy figured she did.

She mooched about in her handbag for the key and opened the front door. He stepped straight in behind her and just for a moment she wondered if she'd done the right thing.

She took off her coat and hung it up.

"The lounge is through there. Make yourself comfortable."

He took off his jacket and threw it on the stairs, pushing her against the wall of the hallway.

"This will do nicely."

"Take this off!"

He tugged at her blouse and she ripped at the buttons and pulled it off, slithering out of her skirt at the same time. Michael pinned her arms above her head and covered her mouth with his to silence the shrieks and yelps, the curses and profanities.

"You know you love it."

He pushed his hand between her legs and forced his fingers under the crotch of the black camisole. Her wetness belied her protestations and her body began to melt into his in capitulation.

"We're home," she whispered.

"Ready to start again Mrs Johnson?"

Lucy looked into her husband's eyes and saw the man she'd married. How had they almost let it slip away?

"Ready to start again," she murmured.

He took her hand and led her upstairs. When you're right at the bottom, the only way is up.

Heartbreak Hotel

"....and forsaking all others be faithful to her as long as you both shall live?"

My lovely Lizzie turned and ran as the vicar's words echoed round the church.

She ran past the organist who huffed and puffed in astonishment; past her sister who gaped, open-mouthed; past the photographer – and then, as suddenly as she had turned the joyful afternoon into an unexpected farce, Lizzie stopped running and slowly turned and faced me. The air was heavy with silence as she stood completely motionless and stared. Just stared. Cringing with embarrassment and sadness, I looked pleadingly at her, willing her to come back. Only her eyes moved. She had the look of a rabbit caught in the headlights. And then she ran again and I pursued her. I had to free her from her fear, whatever it was.

Outside, in the hot sunshine, she sank to her knees and buried her face in her hands. I held her, comforted her, whispering softly:

"Steady on babe. You'll make yourself poorly and that would never do, not today!"

"I can't do it."

"It's just nerves. Take a deep breath and we'll go back in."

"I can't. I can't trust you. I thought I could put it behind me – but I can't. You'll never change."

"I don't understand."

I'd never given her any reason to doubt me. I just couldn't understand what all this was about.

By this time, we had a small audience, consisting of her mother and father and her two sisters. They went into a whispering huddle which didn't include me. I decided the best thing to do was to go back into church and wait for her. She'd soon calm down.

Lizzie's sister walked to the altar and whispered in my ear. Then the whispers passed around the church in Chinese style, the gasps of the recipients getting louder and louder. The rest of the afternoon was a blur of voices and faces, none of them hers. Red, angry faces with pursed lips; sad faces moist with tears; puzzled faces with mouths hanging open like question marks. The voices bounced around the church like war drums. There may have been softer, less accusing words but they were drowned out by the wolves baying for blood.

And now here I was, alone in our honeymoon hotel. I'd decided to come anyway and stay for the week we'd booked. I wondered if she'd turn up.

The answer to that question came in the form of a letter delivered to my room as I lay on the bed, smoking my way through the hundreds of 'what ifs' and 'maybes' that threatened to suffocate me.

I read and re-read the letter. It was terse and uncompromising. No matter how many times I read it, I could find no nuance of emotion or regret, only admonishment and disappointment. I knew that there could be no going back. And now I knew why.

*****

We'd had a good lunch. I could still remember the green of her dress and her eyes; the curves; the intimate stare, her eyes boring holes into my forehead. We shared a bottle of red wine – and then another. We'd staggered back to her room, giggling and expectant. I'd climbed into her body and stayed there for the whole afternoon, eating and drinking her, oblivious to everything except the feast. We'd been one, wrapped up in pure lust.

When the sun went down, we became two again, rolling apart and dropping off the mattress onto the carpet. Seeing her, thin as a stick and sagging breasts, I turned my back and looked for my clothes. Her green dress lay next to my trousers, stained with red wine and the other business of the afternoon. I cursed the red wine and my weakness. I felt a deep sense of shame and wondered how Lizzie's day was going. I was looking forward to making her my second wife. I loved her deeply and knew that I wouldn't make the same mistakes again.

It was difficult to say where my first marriage all went wrong. There was no particular moment, no incident, no animosity. Looking back, I suppose that we'd' been too young. Lust was love, sex was commitment and marriage was an inevitability. We'd drifted apart amicably and done it all again with other people. In my case, I'd done it all again several times, without the impediment of marriage and the expectation of fidelity. My women were always the same sort. Easy come, easy go. Good time girls with pretty faces, mouths as big as their vaginas and brains focused on nothing but the giving and receiving of gratification.

And that had suited me very well.

Until I met Lizzie. We didn't meet in the usual sort of place. No music blaring, no enveloping aroma of fag smoke and yesterday's beer. She was a breath of fresh air and innocence and I couldn't get enough of her. I found her one morning. She was sitting at the desk next to mine at Pitmore's Estate Agents where I worked my cobblers off trying to sell the homes of deserted wives who didn't really want to sell them to anxious-looking young men who didn't really want to buy them.

Lizzie had a well-scrubbed look and her perfume was light and feminine and laced with traces of fabric conditioner. She wore pretty blouses and smart skirts, kitten heels and American Tan tights.

She was everything that my other women hadn't been. She was everything I'd ever wanted.

I'd asked her to marry me six months after we met. I felt as though we had known each other for ever.

We'd planned our wedding together. It was exactly what we wanted. No ostentation or vulgarity. She wore a simple dress in ivory organza, with a modest boat necked style. The bodice was decorated with seed pearls and the skirt hung elegantly from her tiny waist. She might have been a porcelain doll, fragile and delicate, in need of love and care. And as she walked towards me on her father's arm, I made a silent vow that I would love and care for her forever.

And now she was gone.

I'd known her for just 1 year. One year in which universe? Had I known her for 1 seconds or for 100 years? For the blink of an eye or for an aeon of blue moons? We'd shared so much – more than we could ever have imagined; more than we should have wished for.

We were one and yet we were Yin and Yang.

I was the light of optimism that all would be well; she was the dark clouds that hid the future and clung to the darkness of the past.

Maybe she didn't want to see the light. It seemed that whenever there was doubt she found comfort in the familiarity of the blackness. Perhaps she was afraid that the light would shine into the crevices and cracks of our relationship, the imperfections which make us human and give us the capacity for true love.

She was right when she said that I love women. I loved the taste of their flesh and the smell of their desire. To hold a woman in my arms was to feast at a banquet of lust where my senses were bombarded with the vulgarity of plenty.

But now my needs were different. Morning cuddles, holding hands, the softness of her skin and the way she smiled – they satisfied a deeper desire which had been crying out for her.

Meeting my first wife for old times' sake had been a mistake. I'd anticipated a leisurely lunch and a philosophical farewell to the turbulence of my old life in anticipation of calm seas and sunny skies. She'd booked a room at the Red Lion She ordered a bottle of red wine, and then another and in the haze of a 1982 Beaujolais she became a good time girl with a pretty face and a mouth as big as her vagina. I was glad my life was about to change forever.

And now as I lay alone, I knew that things could never be different. I was who I was – and perhaps I wanted it no other way.

Heaven or Hell

"It's surprising, really, just how many different shades of red there are – and choosing the right one is absolutely crucial to the finished effect. Let's try this one ... *Hot Pepper*. No, I don't think so. Far too over-stated. Ah, this is the one .... Here we go .... *Sunset* – that's it. Perfect. Just let me blot those lovely lips and then I'll concentrate on the cheekbones. There's no doubt about it, your face is just wonderful and those cheekbones are your best feature aren't they Janie?

That's what they told me when I was in the modelling business. A model's best asset, they said and I asked them if I could insure them for a couple of million – like Greta Garbo did her legs. Don't think so, darling, they said. You're not likely to break your cheekbones, are you sweetheart? Not unless some jealous bitch comes up and smashes you in the face. There was lots of 'green eye' in the modelling game – they don't call it the cat walk for nothing! Hissing and spitting about everything - who'd pinched whose mascara; who'd been shagged by Romani; whose sequins were gold-plated! It was another world, another life. But I've tried to maintain standards! Never start the day without my full make up and a dousing in Christian Dior. I suppose it's called 'keeping up appearances' isn't it?

D'you know what I mean? That's why I enjoy my work so much. Making women look their best. It's incredibly challenging and fulfilling – it's amazing the number of people who've said to me "God, I've never seen her look so good!"

I've painted you up and done your hair and your husband will be thrilled when he sees you. I have to say that you look pretty stunning. Good heavens! I can't believe how much I've rabbited on since you arrived. Practically told you my whole life story, I have! You haven't got a word in edgeways!"

Gary rang the bell and peered through the door. Marcia let him in.

"She looks gorgeous – but she's not quite ready yet. Take a seat."

She hurried back into the beauty parlour at the rear. She was most insistent that her clients had total privacy.

He sank into a leather sofa and studied the wall art. It was salacious to say the least. The images were erotic in spite of their unusual settings. Fascinating. He wondered if Janie would earn a place in the line-up. His wife was a beautiful woman and to have her immortalised up there among the 'crème de la crème' would be a dream come true.

Marcia came out into the waiting room and held up two basques, one red, one white. She grinned.

"Heaven or hell? Your choice."

Gary walked towards the red one which was in Marcia's left hand. Was it heaven or was it hell? He closed his eyes.

It was the red one she wore when she rode him like the devil's whore, spitting and hissing. Red for whipping, biting. Red hot tongues intertwining and faces dripping with brimstone. The deeper he entered her, the more she raged against him and the deeper he travelled until they were both suffocated. They wanted to come back but could not until it was over. And then, as quickly as it had begun, it was finished and his ejaculation restored coolness and calm and they were themselves again - whoever they were.

He touched the white one, fingering it, not wanting to damage it or mark it with his grubbiness but needing to touch it. It was her innocence and fidelity. The purity of her love. The softness of her skin. She was the good girl with the bad guy just wanting gentleness and the slow strokes of a bow across a violin, creating new beginnings. No prejudice. Just an awareness of the simplicity of what they had. No emotional baggage. No inner critic. The clarity of purpose with no hidden agenda. An angel protecting their safety and happiness."

"The white one."

Marcia smiled. "She'll be with you in a minute."

Moments later Marcia called him and Gary made his way into the beauty parlour. He approached Janie and stroked her cheek tenderly. It was as cold as ice. He kissed her soft red lips and felt the chill of the breath of death. He wept hot tears of anguish and loss. But he knew that even the salt of his tears could preserve nothing but her memory. She was gone.

"God, I've never seen her look so good! But how do you do a job like this?"

"A job's a job, isn't it? I just pretend they're still alive – that they're friends of mine. Takes my mind off it. I do enjoy the work, believe it or not – and I need the money, of course!"

Gary walked out into the January afternoon and pulled up his collar against the bitter wind. Yesterday's snow was staring him stubbornly in the face and threatening to turn to ice as the temperature dropped.

Hell had frozen over.

In Thoughts of You

The sun is shining and the day depressingly bright and cheerful with more than a hint of impertinent normality. There are no spaces outside the crematorium so I decide park round the corner outside a pub. A Skol lager can rolls defiantly into the gutter and challenges me to flatten it. I refuse and stop the car just short of its intended destination. Skol. I smile wanly, remembering the last funeral I went to.

As my father's coffin had disappeared into the muddy hole in the ground, a silence descended on the assembly of family and friends. An embarrassed, uncomfortable silence that said: "What shall we do now?" Twelve pairs of eyes stared at twelve pairs of shiny black shoes, then gazed upwards to check whether there was any sign at all that our father was in heaven, as the priest had just so righteously claimed. It soon became apparent that not only was he there, but he'd sent a message. Hovering above us in a cloudless sky was an airship – one of the sort that tows an advertising banner at special events. Skol. Just the one word. The twelve pairs of eyes narrowed in disbelief and stifled mirth at the unspoken recollection of the remainder of the slogan: Skol ...... time for a sharp exit! That was the last time that I heard silence that day. A chorus of tittering rose to a crescendo and turned the occasion into what it should have been. He always knew how to break the ice.

Funny how memories stick in one's subconscious mind and rear their heads so much later, poking their noses into the present and sniffing at the detritus of the past. Memories oxygenate the mind, clearing the debris of broken promises, shattered dreams and fraught emotions. Memories re-write history. They provide tangible evidence that life continues after death; that trust can follow betrayal; that all is never lost, merely temporarily mislaid. Memories trigger other memories and either shoot them dead or change their form and shape. A memory today will not be the same as it was yesterday and tomorrow it will be different again. Memories are totally unreliable but it is this unreliability which makes them such an essential part of the human survival kit. We can use them as we wish. The same memory can provide an opportunity for quiet reflection or inane hilarity. It can spark a moment of deep grief or unimagined joy.

I glance at the overflowing bin where the can belongs. It vomits pizza boxes, left-over take-aways and other evidence of life's essentials.

I shudder with distaste. The garbage shudders back and eyes up my smart coat, making me feel uncomfortable and out of place. As I get out of the car, it starts to rain and I scuttle into the pub doorway. The door rattles open and the stink of beer, burgers and the bullshit of conviviality tumbles through, followed by a voice

"Mornin' darlin'. Been waiting long?"

Startled, I turn round and am not surprised to see that The Voice looks as rough as it sounds.

"Waiting?"

"For a drink?"

"No. No thanks. I'm just getting my umbrella sorted and I'll be out of your way."

He eyes up my black coat and matching accessories.

"Going to the crem?"

"Yes. I am actually."

"I'll be going across myself in a minute or two. Got to give Ruthey a good send off."

"You knew her well?"

"She used to come in here in here every day. Liked a couple of gin and tonics and a bit of a chat. Interesting woman."

I could see past The Voice into the bar and the thought of Ruth slumming it in this place painted a picture which I'd rather not imagine.

"She lived round here then?"

"Yep. In the maisonettes opposite Green Park."

The rain had stopped. I figured I had time to walk round to the park. I wanted to see where Ruth had ended up.

We'd met when we at university and became good friends. We supported each other through the thick and thin of failed job interviews, broken relationships and everything in between. We'd shared beds on wild holidays in Tenerife and shared secrets over tea, cheese toasties and tortillas.

It had been over a cup of tea and a toasted sandwich in Leamington that Ruth had confided in me that she thought her husband was having an affair. She'd met Doug in her first job as a newly-qualified teacher. He was Head of Science and he'd taken Ruth under his wing. They dated, got engaged and married within the year. Their wedding was a splendid affair with flowery hats, flowing speeches and fiddly food. Ruth couldn't have been happier. This was her dream come true.

It wasn't my sort of wedding. If it had to be done, I favoured the quick dash to the registry office and 'pie and a pint' approach but then the subject of weddings hadn't been an issue for me when Ruth got married. I was a die-hard career girl. I had no intention of getting shackled. I wanted sole ownership of the remote control, my toilet seat and my holiday destinations. That didn't mean to say that men were out of the question; they just weren't part of any long-term plan. They came and they went.

Green Park belied its name. It was largely devoid of trees and shrubs and was dominated by a run-down children's play area. Patches of grass fought for survival amid the muddy tyre marks, condoms and dirty syringes, the shit of despair. The maisonettes overlooked the park, standing guard over their territory, hearing all, seeing all but telling little. Grubby washing strung across their balconies publically airing their owners' secrets without an atom of shame; torn curtains at the windows concealed nothing, sleeping dogs were not let lie but instead prodded and goaded into barking and fighting. The smell of neglect and destruction epitomised the hopelessness which defined the lives of those who existed in this place.

I wept for Ruth and for what had brought her here.

I wanted to go home.

An hour later, I was back in my apartment in Hampstead. I made a coffee and, still in my black dress and stiletto heels, perched on the chair by the window. I gazed through the window as I had so many times before. But this time I couldn't focus on the familiar scene. Instead, smart houses had lighted windows and closed doors. Made-up faces of fashionistas were masks concealing all but their features. There was no dirty washing aired in Hamsptead, only the obscenity of wealth, privilege and ill-gotten gains.

I thought about Ruth and our student days; Ruth and her wedding day; Ruth and her happiness with her beloved husband. I thought about Doug and what he'd had with Ruth and how he could have betrayed her when she loved him so much.

I was so ashamed. I trembled with sadness and regret. Doug had become a part of my life two years after he and Ruth were married. He came. He went. Back to Ruth. Back to me. But one day he came to me and never went home again. Doug and I had our quick dash to the registry office and our pie and a pint and lived happily never after with his choice of TV entertainment, his pee on the toilet seat and holidays on exotic beaches where he could admire the boobs and bums.

They say that when a man marries his mistress he creates a vacancy. That vacancy was filled when Doug met the next love of his life. One day he never came home and I knew that I had only myself to blame.

Just Another Day

The woman peered at the letter which had just been thrust in her direction. The air was thick with curses and exasperation. Sensing the approaching storm, she glanced anxiously at Simon. Head in hands, he squatted on the floor and clenched his teeth in undiluted anger.

Simon wrote novels – well, to be precise, he wrote one novel, over and over again. He lived in the attic flat at the top of her Edwardian house.

"Not again! I can't believe it! I could paper the walls with the rejection slips. I'm totally knackered. Sleep deprivation is the curse of the writer. When I'm not worrying about what I've written, I'm worrying about what I haven't written. Is it better to write literary fiction badly or to write pulp fiction well? Is it appropriate to sacrifice one's principles for the sake of paying the bills? My head is full of split infinitives and paltry plots."

Day after day Simon tortured himself with his dilemma and the woman did all she could to reassure him. She'd hug him and squeeze his hand.

"Try not to worry, Simon. Things will get better. It's not the end of the world. It's just another day."

She became his close friend and confidante and his need for a woman like her was clear for all to see. No-one could call him good-looking but yet he had an air of attractiveness which beguiled her. Every time she looked at him, she loved him more than she had the day before; more than she had loved her father; more than she had loved all the people she had loved. And there had been so many. The woman, in turn, was popular with everyone. She was a thoroughly pleasant woman, good looking enough - but not so good-looking that she'd be tempted to stray. Prospective mothersin-law adored her for her kindness, her child-bearing hips and her good old-fashioned common sense.

Within the year, they were married. Life just got better and better. She helped him with his writing, made suggestions when he re-drafted his work, contacted literary agents on his behalf.

His writing became as important to her as it was to him. She talked endlessly with her friends about the merits of literary fiction and the trash of formulaic pulp. The woman, who had read very little in the way of the great classics, spoke with conviction of the plotted novels of Charles Dickens and the works of the Modernists. She repeated the ideas and sentiments of her husband without difficulty, for she had none of her own on any subject. Her understanding of the world was one provided by her father after her mother had left them.

Married life suited the woman and she became happier by the day. She cooked cottage pie and chicken casserole, kept the house spick and span and ironed Simon's shirts with meticulous precision.

"I love you so much," she would say, "that it hurts."

Just after their first wedding anniversary, he went to London to see his agent.

She had never spent a night without him before and sleep did not come easily. She missed the reassuring warmth of his body next to hers. She felt as though a part of her was missing. When the loss became too much to bear, she got up and sat by the window, waiting to be made whole again.

Dawn came not with the rosy glow of a new day but with a flashing blue light and the news that Simon was dead. A motorway pile-up.

The woman realised that she would never be whole again, that this desperate loss would be a part of her life forever. Friends feared for her as she tried to seek Simon in death. A cocktail of anti-depressants and brandy left her barely alive and in a fog of grief from which there seemed no escape. Friends took turns to stay with her.

"When will the pain go away?" she'd sob, day in, day out. And they'd shake their heads in sadness at the pity of it all.

A few months later, the pain was less and she set about dealing with some of the practicalities that living brings. She must try to put the past behind her. After all, this was just another day. She needed a car. She put on her black coat, her black boots and red hat and picked up her new red handbag which had been a present from Simon. Lowering her eyes, she made her way briskly along the embankment to the used-car garage at the other end of town. The cars looked good considering they weren't new. The salesman looked quite smart himself, considering that he was selling second-hand cars. He wore an expensive suit, which wasn't shiny; he had a kind smile, which wasn't phoney. He asked her whether she was OK. She supposed he made small talk with all his customers - that this was just another day in the life of a used-car salesman. His voice was quite cultured and he seemed to be well-educated, considering that he was just a car salesman. He listened sympathetically as, dabbing her eyes and biting her lip until it bled, she told him of her reduced circumstances.

"Nil desperandum, Madam. There, there! Time to move on."

He ushered her towards a gleaming ice-blue mini and wound himself up into a frenzy of enthusiasm. Staccato phrases tumbled from his lips as he extolled the virtues of the car which would change her life forever.

"10,000 miles on the clock. Genuine mileage. One lady owner …"

After a while, she became aware that she had stopped listening and that his deep brown eyes were occupying her complete attention.

The eyes stayed with her long after she had left the showroom, having purchased the ice-blue mini. It was hard to say which was the most irresistible, the car or Alan Clarke of *Clarke's Quality Motors – Even Lovelier the Second Time Around*. What was certain, however, was that her decision to buy the car did indeed change her life forever in a way which Alan Clarke did not intend.

A few days after buying the car, the woman's memories of the velvet voice and chocolate eyes were tainted by a faulty carburetor which led her to consider for a moment that Alan Clarke may not be what he seemed. She took the car to a garage and was soon persuaded that the fault was intermittent and that the car was a really 'good buy'. The reputation of Alan Clarke remained similarly unblemished, for he was well-known in the town:

"He's a good, reliable, honest chap," asserted the garage man, "The sort you'd buy a second-hand car from. His business is doing really well. I hear he's looking for someone to do some office work."

The garage man smiled broadly and the woman was not slow to take the hint. News travelled fast in the small town and it was common knowledge that she was finding it hard to make ends meet.

Two days later, she was sitting, quite 'at home', in the office of *Clarke's Quality Motors* and, within months, Alan Clarke was her husband and installed with similar comfort in her king-sized bed in her elegant house. They made the perfect couple and she had never been happier or more in love. She could not look at him without a swell of pride and joy and she felt a stab of delight when other women glanced at him with more than a passing interest. Days were spent at the showroom, building up the business and evenings were a round of dinner parties, clubs and visits to the theatre with Alan's friends – or 'business associates' as he called them. She didn't see much of her own friends now. Sometimes they would call her for a chat and she would talk endlessly of the world of used cars. Her husband saw the business as making a major contribution to the sustainability agenda and she took on this view as though it were her own original thought:

"No-one should be allowed to buy a new car," she would say, "until they have owned at least three used cars. It's the ultimate in recycling. It's so obvious. It's unthinkable that the government isn't ahead of the game."

She became obsessed with brake pads, oil filters, spark plugs and profit margins and studied their relevance with the same fervour that she had once applied to participles and oxymorons.

Her friends at the Book Circle tried to persuade her to come back to the weekly meetings and even tempted her by including one of her favourite authors on the reading list.

"What use was Thomas Hardy in the real world?" she exclaimed scornfully. "What did he contribute to industry, to the economy, to the world we live in today?" Her husband loathed books – and all the arts – and she wholeheartedly agreed with him.

And so their life went on comfortably and harmoniously. They never had a cross word. Whatever pleased him pleased her; when he was happy, she was happy too. The happier she was, the more she loved him and the more she loved him, the happier she was. And he was happy, too, and loved her dearly. She worked harder and harder in the business. When they entertained, she cooked lamb shanks in red wine and shallots and crème Brule. She dressed impeccably and there was never a hair out of place as they glided across the dance floor at the Armani Club.

One evening as he locked up the showroom, Alan was attacked and robbed. So severe were his injuries that he was hospitalised for seven weeks. The woman prayed constantly for his recovery. She realised that if he didn't recover she would never be whole again, that this desperate loss would be a part of her life forever

A young doctor was a lodger in their house. He had the attic flat where Simon had lived before they'd got together. It had been a mutually convenient arrangement – he'd needed somewhere to live after his wife had thrown him out; she'd needed the extra money in those days. During the long weeks of Alan's absence, he'd often call in to see her, to ask about his progress. He was good company. They'd have a drink and sometimes watch television for an hour or so. He needed the company as much as she did and she was such a good listener. He'd talk to her about how much he missed his little boy. His wife wouldn't allow him to see the boy although he sent her money every month. It was a sad state of affairs and the woman felt depressed at the sadness of it all and was so sorry for Dr Arnold. She thought about what her husband would say if he were here. Alan was such a sensible, decent man. Always did the right thing. She was sure that he'd say: "Come on, old chap! Why not try to patch things up with your wife? Make a go of it – for the sake of the child." So, whenever Dr Arnold popped in to see her, her parting words would always be:

"Thank you so much for your kindness. Why not try to patch things up with your wife? Make a go of it – for the sake of the child."

She was glad when Alan came back home. She had so much to tell him. She told him about Dr Arnold's son and how much the doctor missed him and her husband said:

"Why doesn't he try to patch things up with his wife? Make a go of it – for the sake of the child."

And as they spoke of the child and of the doctor's deep love for his son, they considered too how their own love could be augmented by a child and how they could be even happier than they were now.

Five years passed by and the clinics and the treatments yielded no results. The couple became reconciled to the reality of their situation and continued their lives in quiet contentment. To their neighbours and friends they were the personification of 'lived happily ever after'. But alas they were not. Each day was the same as the last. Just another day.

Alan began to have dreadful headaches and, without warning, dropped dead one winter's morning as he set off for work. The woman was alone again. She was devastated and totally bereft. She sobbed and wailed, hour after hour, night and day. Sometimes she'd eat a slice of toast or a chocolate biscuit, washed down with glasses of dry white wine. She was soon a shadow of the woman she had been.

"I'm nobody without him," she would cry. "I've nothing left to live for." She realised that she would never be whole again, that this desperate loss would be a part of her life forever.

Her friends tried their best, but gradually lost patience. She wouldn't help herself. Only the doctor comforted her in the privacy of her king-size bed in her elegant house; only she and the doctor knew the nature of that comfort for they had decided they must be discreet.

Their secret remained safe until one day in the supermarket the woman met a neighbour who sold tea and buns at the local hospital:

"Do you know just how much MRSA there is in that hospital? There were twenty new cases just last week. It's proven that the alcohol hand-gels are ineffective against these bacteria and that only the use of soap and water will eliminate the spread of this wretched super-bug. New procedures are to be introduced with immediate effect."

And so the pillow talk of the doctor and the woman became the sole subject of her conversation. It was the talk of the town and people began to draw the conclusions which the couple had dreaded would become common knowledge. As their relationship blossomed, she became her old self and people began to like her again. She and the doctor entertained his friends and colleagues and she would join in happily with their conversations, keen to show an interest in his work. She spoke eruditely of government targets for the reduction of Type II Diabetes, of the effects of beta-blockers on erectile dysfunction and of the expected influenza pandemic. This irritated and embarrassed the doctor so much that there would always be a row after their guests had left.

"You make me cringe, woman. Why can't you stick to what you know instead of butting in?"

"But what do I know? What would you like me to talk about?" she would ask and she would cry inconsolably and cling to him, trembling and anxious. And he would hug her and apologise for his anger and all would be well again. Every time she looked at him, she loved him more than she had the day before; more than she had loved her father; more than she had loved all the people she had loved.

But something changed. The doctor stopped inviting his friends around and before the year was out he had obtained a post in a town in Scotland and the woman was left alone again.

She sank into a depression far deeper than any she had suffered before. She began to neglect herself and on the few occasions that she ventured out, people could barely recognise the unkempt, bedraggled specimen of humanity who staggered down the street clutching bottles of wine and cans of beans. The woman realised that she would never be whole again, that this desperate loss would be a part of her life forever.

She sat in the dusty house amid piles of books, magazines and periodicals – but her interest in the cost of a used Jaguar was neither more nor less than that of her desire to read her favourite poetry anthology or to scrutinise the lists of adverse drug reactions which plopped still through her letterbox long after the doctor had left. She was interested in nothing. She asked no questions – of herself or of others – and therefore she got no answers. She knew nothing and cared little that her brain served no purpose other than to sustain her existence. Each breaking dawn brought just another day.

She found the child one day on her way home from the Off Licence. He was wandering in the road. He smiled at her and when she held out her hand he grasped it and she knew it was meant to be. She took him home and made him beans on toast and a mug of cocoa. He seemed hungry. A good job she'd found him when she had. She took off his grubby clothes and wrapped him in a blanket. He slept soundly in her bed throughout the night and when he awoke he threw his arms around her neck. He spoke little – except to tell the woman that he had run away. She did not ask from whom or from where or for what reason. It didn't matter. He was with her now. He was where he belonged.

She was so delighted at the thought of a happy ending for the little boy who needed a stable family life. She felt privileged to bestow such a gift!

In no time at all, the woman and the house and the boy were scrubbed clean and restored to their former glory. There was no trace of the past.

The woman took to the boy as though he were her own child. She loved him so much that her heart ached. He was such a handsome boy. Such a wonderful temperament. He was perfect. Every time she looked at him, she loved him more than she had the day before; more than she had loved her father; more than she had loved all the people she had loved.

She took care of his every need. Nothing was too much trouble. Every evening, after their meal, they sat at the big table in the kitchen and they worked together on arithmetic and reading and writing. The woman was astonished at his knowledge and intelligence.

"A square number is the product of two identical numbers" he told her as he worked through a page of math's exercises.

"Product?" she raised an eyebrow of enquiry.

"The answer when you multiply two numbers. So, 36 is a square number."

"Of course." She smiled knowingly. "A square number is the product of two identical numbers"

For the first time in many years, the woman was interested in something. She had asked a question and received an answer. She glowed. It was her opinion that 81 was a square number and she told the boy so.

She was so proud of him. They lived in their own little world. They needed only each other. The world outside was a hostile place. You couldn't be too careful. The traffic was appalling – and so many strangers. She would die if anything happened to him. He meant the world to her.

At the end of the day, after she'd fed him, they'd sit together in front of the fire and she'd talk to him. She told him about the plotted novels of Charles Dickens and the works of the Modernists. She talked of the sustainability agenda with enthusiasm.

"No-one should be allowed to buy a new car," she told him, "until they have owned at least three used cars. It's the ultimate in recycling. It's so obvious. It's unthinkable that the government isn't ahead of the game."

She showed him pictures of brake pads, oil filters and spark plugs. She read to him from the newspaper about the challenges faced by the NHS.

The boy would look at her in astonishment, his eyes agog,

"You know so many things. I wonder if I'll ever be as clever as you. Is there anything you don't know?"

The woman hugged the boy and held him close. This was not just another day. This day was so special. Every time she looked at him, she knew more and more – more than she had the day before; more than she had in her childhood, more than she had on any day of her life. And there had been so many.

Lazy Hazy Days

Helen saw the man approach her bed. It was definitely him. He'd come back for her. That was typical of him. Totally reliable, dependable, exuding warmth and strength. The summer of 1952. He used to wait for her in the same place, every day - same time, same place. He was part of the scenery, leaning against his bike, in such a natural way, smiling. Skin weathered, eyes twinkling.

Helen trembled with emotion as she caught sight of him. Tears rose and stung her eyes as she relived the anguish of their separation. They'd dragged her away, torn her from him, kicking and screaming. The law was on their side, they said. No point in objecting or protesting. He wasn't right for any girl, especially her. He was just a fairground gypsy. No future. No morals. No finesse. No fixed abode. No. No. No.

Now he was back and life would begin again, more fragrant and more poignant than before. And every day, come rain or shine, he'd walk to meet her, just as he did before and lean against his bike, waiting. She'd wear her red dress and white stilettos and curl her hair. Same time, same place. She needs him. She loves him and he loves her. And the lazy hazy days of summer belong to them now and nothing can change that.

She peered at him through the shadows of her memory and hoped she wasn't mistaken. Was it him? It surely was. Deep brown eyes and pearly teeth; all dressed up like a dog's dinner, topped with a fetching panama.

Helen's heart pounded and she broke into a sweat. The face came nearer and she screamed out loud. She didn't know this man. His eyes were grey and matched his hair. He was wearing a mask.

She called for her mother but she was back home in London where the bombs were dropping. Her mum had said that Helen was here to be safe. Away from the bombs. Was this what safe was? Helen wanted her own bed. She didn't like this one. She wanted a saggy mattress and her little brother putting his cold feet against hers and telling her stories about the Germans.

Helen hit out at the man leaning over her:

"Bugger off, Mr Hitler. You're not wanted here."

"Calm down Mrs Roberts. You're in hospital. You had a fall and fractured your hip. You're going to have an operation to mend it."

She could still hear his voice. She'd told him to bugger off but he was still there. Helen was feeling rather strange. She knew that she was about to go down the long tunnel and fall down the rabbit hole ... ...

She was feeling stranger by the minute. This place was packed with people. They were standing round a figure lying on a table.

"I wonder if I've been changed in the night. Let me think. Was I the same when I got up this morning? I almost think I can remember feeling a little different. But if I'm not the same, the next question is 'Who in the world am I?' Ah, that's the great puzzle!"

"We're all mad here!"

"Explain yourself"

"I can't explain myself, I'm afraid, Sir, because I'm not myself you see."

"Off with her head."

"But then, shall I never get any older than I am now? That'll be a comfort in one way but then I still have lessons to learn."

"What is the use of repeating all that stuff, if you don't explain it as you go on? It's by far the most confusing thing I ever heard! Begin at the beginning and go on till you come to the end: then stop."

And so Helen began to tell the rabbit in the white mask all about it. She didn't start at the beginning though. She started at Christmas. Any Christmas. They were all the same. She told him about the Christmases of her childhood. She supposed that Christmas had always been about visitors – shepherds, grandsons, great grandchildren. In those days, you couldn't move in their house for visitors. All came round in the evening, they did, on Christmas Day. Cold turkey sandwiches and a sing-song round the piano. Mum and Dad loved having a houseful. Can't have a proper Christmas without family. That's what Dad used to say. He was a real family man was Dad. That's what made it so hard ......

Helen's eyes stung with tears as she thought back to the bitterness of his words:

"You've made your bed, our Helen, now you'll lie on it. And it won't be in this house. This is a decent house. We've made the arrangements. We'll take you to St. Hilda's next Monday – on the train. Mother Therese is expecting you at lunch time. Do as you're told and you'll be alright. They won't stand no messing, mind. Stop crying. There's been enough tears, our Helen. When it's all over, you can go and stay with Aunt Beattie. She's arranging some work for you. And that's an end to it."

And then - Christmas 19 something or other ...every Christmas was the same. Festival of Readings and Carols on Radio 3. The music blared on in the background and the reader spoke, with a nonchalance which was breathtaking to Helen, of King Herod's appalling plans to murder the baby Jesus. Helen had gulped and looked towards the crib which sat on the small table between the Christmas tree and the wireless. At least he was safe here with her.

You'd do anything to keep them safe. You'd kill anyone who tried to hurt them or take them away. That's why I did it. I kicked Mother Therese. I kicked and screamed and threw the pen and the papers at her. The orderlies rushed in and pinned my arms behind my back and pushed me onto the floor. And when I'd run out of breath and I couldn't scream anymore, I cowered like a sick animal in the corner of my cell, sobbing. Mother Therese towered over me, jabbing her pointed chin – a giant evil crow, spitting out words like seeds surplus to requirements."

Helen re-lived the scene each Christmas: Mother Therese had told her that they didn't need her sort there; that she was upsetting the other girls; that she'd either pick up the pen and sign the papers or they'd contact the asylum. The asylum ... the asylum! The words had bounced off the walls and punched her in the chest and she'd gasped for breath and gasped again as she'd closed her eyes and remembered the first time she'd ever heard the word. She must have been about ten. She'd heard Siobhan Murphy, from down the street, howling like a banshee. Helen had run down the garden path with her mother beside her and they'd watched her being dragged off and mum had said: 'She's going to the asylum. Lost her head, she has. Gone doo-lalley.' And Helen had told Mother Therese, in no uncertain terms, that she wasn't doo-lalley and that she wasn't going to the asylum.

But Helen's spirit had been no match for the terrible threats of Mother Therese, who promised Helen that if she didn't do as she was told, she'd be locked up for ever – for the rest of her time on earth – and that then she'd rot in hell for her sins. With the naivety of youth, Helen had asked her if she'd still go to hell even if she signed the papers, or would she be forgiven. This question had sent the black crow into a paroxysm of rage and her eyes had bulged as she'd proclaimed that it would be a long time before Helen would be forgiven for the shame and disgrace that she'd brought on herself and her baby, and her poor mother and father and the holy Mother Church.

Helen trembled and on the Christmas card which Helen held, the virgin's face shone brightly, her eyes smiled kindly and her head seemed to nod wisely.

The rabbit in the white mask smiled.

"If I had a world of my own," she told him, "everything would be nonsense. Nothing would be what it is, because everything would be what it isn't. And contrary wise, what is, it wouldn't be. And what it wouldn't be, it would. You see?"

He nodded. And a dark haired girl in a red dress and white stilettos threw a bicycle into the sea and waved to a panama which was bobbing up and down helplessly on the waves, getting smaller and smaller as it travelled towards the horizon. The lazy hazy days were over.

Man Pursued

A pile of blood and feathers carpet the ground, the over-stated gore of the blood contrasting sharply with the white innocence of feathers. In the corner of the coop, a dead chicken lies featherless, its skin bearing the evidence of recent plucking. Its neck is stretched like over-used chewing gum. Its bulging eyes, unseeing, stare at the only other living occupant of the coop.

Ben stares down at the chicken, agitated and yet triumphant. He meets its gaze. His eyes are glazed and similarly unseeing. He raises his arms in a gesture of pride and joy and opens his mouth wide in a silent scream.

Oliver sits at his desk which is strewn with the clutter and paraphernalia of a disorganised writer. He stubs out a cigarette into an overflowing ashtray and pours himself a drink from a half-empty whisky bottle. He peers at a computer screen and rubs his eyes, then glances at his watch, sighing deeply.

The scene in the chicken coop is frozen onto the computer screen. It is as if the lifelessness of the chicken is permeating the room.

Oliver's mouth begins to move as he peers at the words and begins to read them. He reads from the screen, scratching his head and leaning back in his seat.

> "I killed a chicken. I trapped it
> in a corner and I wrung its neck.
> It was the first chicken I'd ever
> killed..."

He stops dead in his tracks, as if he is too horrified to read on. He looks like someone who is reading this for the first time and is surprised at its content.

Ben moves away from the lifeless chicken and towards what appears to be another mutilated bird in the corner of the coop. As the 'bird' comes into close-up, it takes on a vaguely human form. Its legs are trussed up and tied with string and yet, strangely, it is still wearing a pair of Reebok trainers on its feet. The body is otherwise unclothed, slit from the pubic area, along the abdomen and beyond the chest.

Oliver's eyes scan the screen and he reads on

"... but I knew how to do it. I've
watched granddad do it loads of
times. So, anyway, I killed the
chicken and got it ready for lunch ... "

He stumbles. He can hardly bear to read it aloud. His head moves from left to right in a gesture of disbelief as he scans the words

The bloody corpse is without the slightest dignity. There is not a hair on its head or body to cover even an inch of the tanned and youthful flesh. Ben picks his way through the innards which are pouring from the gaping wounds, examining the body parts with a detached curiosity. He is apparently oblivious to the horror of the scene or to the pool of blood in which he is sitting. You have to take the innards out - they call them giblets. Anyway, you probably know all this. I can tell that you're a man who knows things.

Oliver puts his head in his hands, lights another cigarette and downs the remainder of the whisky. He searches around on his desk for his phone, hurling papers and books onto the floor in a display of peevish inebriation.

He mutters under his breath.

"But I'm not a man who knows things - not enough things, anyway. Time to phone a friend"

He uncovers his phone with a glee that would have you believe that it had been lost for several weeks. He dials up.

"Hi Sam. ... yeh, I know the time. I'm calling in a favour. I've got this er ... strange guy in my new book. Need some professional advice to bring him to life."

He rocks back in his chair and guffaws with laughter.

"No, he's not dead. He just killed someone else. Eh? No. Too complicated to tell you now. OK -tomorrow? Yeah, fine. 10.15 at the hospital. See you then."

Oliver is not sorry to see the certainty of daylight. He gets out of his car and looks around absent-mindedly. Either he's never been there before or he can't quite remember where he's supposed to go. He shuts the car door but it doesn't quite close. The car is a rusting heap. He gives it a hefty kick and the wing mirror falls off. He picks it up and tosses it onto a grass verge. Unnoticed by Oliver, it lands next to a dead pigeon.

A passing woman sees this and shouts to Oliver. Laughing maniacally.

"He won't be needing no mirror, Mister. He's a gonna! He won't be flying no more, so why would he need a wing mirror?"

Oliver stares at the woman and then looks at the bird. Not a smile crosses his face; not even a flicker. He walks quite briskly into the building, as though his mission was all in a day's work.

Oliver sighs in exasperation. He walks off in high dudgeon, his mind suddenly focused by the realisation that he is probably late. He glances at his watch and breaks into a run.

He's glad to see Sam after all these years and Sam greets him warmly. Wearing an immaculate suit, silver hair and an air of professorial integrity he certainly looks the part. The office is clinically well-organised. It is clearly the office of a psychiatrist. The walls are lined with books relating to all aspects of the human condition. Oliver peers at them hopefully, convinced that in at least one of them, lies the key to Ben's motive for murder.

Sam pours drinks for them both and leans back in his chair.

"So what's the story, Ollie? Who's this guy killed, and why?"

"Well, basically he kills a bloke because he thinks the guy's a chicken."

"Why does he think he's a chicken?"

Sam leans forward and stares at Oliver with the patient gaze of one for whom this sort of conversation is an occupational hazard.

"Because he's ... well ... strange"

"Strange?"

"You know ...."

"No."

"Mentally ill."

"Psychiatrically or emotionally challenged?"

Oliver nods and sighs. He isn't good at PC talk. He'd only just stopped himself from saying 'Bonkers'

"So? So, he's ill. But why does he think the other man's a chicken?"

Oliver shuffles uncomfortably as he begins to realise the limitations of the internet as an 'information super highway'. He puts his hand together in an attitude of prayer, fingers pointing upwards in the shape of a church steeple. He speaks deliberately and slowly, imbuing his words with an air of authority.

"Because ... he is unable to engage with ... reality. He feels as though he's trapped in a bubble. He's a man pursued by his inner self."

Sam raises his eyebrows and leans back in his chair. He stares at Oliver who pouts defiantly, stares back and leans back in his chair, mirroring Sam's body language.

"He's not 'strange', Ollie. Your character may be psychotic or schizophrenic, even criminally insane. But strange – no!

"You haven't even read it. Here, I've highlighted the relevant sections."

Oliver stands up and thrusts a sheaf of disreputably curled-up papers at Sam. Sam leans even further back in his chair and wrinkles his nose in disgust.

"I have no need to read it, Ollie. It's technically inaccurate. You stick to the writing and leave the diagnoses to the shrinks. You need to do more research."

Oliver snatches back the papers and walks over to one of the book shelves. He picks up a hefty tome and begins to flick through it in a frenzied search. Sam swings round on his chair.

"Hey, Ollie. Calm down, man. What is it you want to know? Perhaps I can help."

Oliver puts down the book and walks towards Sam. His movements are slow, deliberate, almost menacing. He clenches his fists and holds them stiffly at his sides. When he speaks, he spits out the words as though he is getting rid of fish bones which have been stuck in his throat for as long as he can remember.

"What sort of man would kill another because he thought he was a chicken? That's what I want to know. Not just kill him, but savage him, mutilate him, butcher him? What sort of man would do that, Dr Samuel Caldwell?"

Oliver sits back down, shakes from head to toe and cries like a baby. Sam pours him another drink and, shaking his head, hands it to him.

"I think you should give up writing, Ollie. When I suggested it, when you had your breakdown, I thought it'd be therapeutic. It's stressing you Ollie. Leave it alone."

Oliver puts down his drink and, his composure regained, speaks quietly and calmly.

"What sort of man, Sam?"

"A very sick man. You can't put the mentally ill into boxes, Ollie, and give each box a label. Psychiatric illnesses are complex. Patients often have features of many different conditions..."

"How can I learn about them?"

"Spend a few days in this place!"

Sam throws back his head and laughs.

"When you leave, you'll know everything you need to know about mental illness. You'll be an A1 chicken-lickin nutter!"

Sam stands up and picks up Oliver's coat, in a not-too subtle attempt to bring the difficult conversation to a close. Oliver stays seated and turns to face Sam. His face is tense and drawn. Sam's little joke has done nothing to lighten the atmosphere.

"When can I do that, Sam?"

Sam, incredulous, puts down Oliver's coat and pours himself a drink. He downs it 'in one' and then strides over to Oliver. His calm bedside manner has evaporated and he is agitated and short-tempered. Oliver repeats the question.

"When? When can I do that, Sam? I need to know?"

"You can't do it. It was a joke for God's sake. You can't be admitted to a psychiatric hospital unless ..."

"... you're mentally ill."

"Correct. And you're not Ollie. You're fully recovered."

Oliver shuffles his feet and stares down at them.

"I could fake it."

Sam resumes his position behind his desk and loosens his tie. Beads of perspiration are forming on his forehead. Working with these people is getting more and more difficult.

"Get this Ollie and get it straight. Have you heard about the David Rosehan Experiment of 1972 ...?"

"... Yeh. I've heard of it. What was it called?"

"It was called On Being Sane in Insane Places – but it was an experiment that couldn't work now. Diagnostic procedures were revised soon afterwards and anyway, everyone in psychiatry knows about Rosehan's stunt."

"I think it can be done. Doctors just can't bring themselves to say 'I don't know' or 'I'm not sure'

"Maybe. But it's not professional arrogance that drives them. They have to believe that their patients are telling the truth ..."

"...the truth as they see it Sam."

"...of course ...in order to help them – as they are obliged to do by the terms of the Hippocratic Oath."

"Then it can be done. I rest my case."

Sam stands up and gives Oliver a farewell pat on the back. He clearly considers the subject well and truly closed. He opens the door and Oliver shuffles out of the room, deep in thought.

"Bye, Ollie. This research of yours must be a matter of life and death!"

"It is, Sam. It is."

"Just don't try it in my hospital. I'm busy with sick people who need me. They wring the shit out of me. The human mind is unpredictable and unfathomable. You can bet your bottom dollar I'll get no sleep tonight. I'm on call. Sam Caldwell at the ready – to sort out the attempted suicides, the overdoses, the senile, the just plain barmy."

Dr Caldwell shuts the door behind him with a sigh of relief. He's more than ready to go home. He picks up his umbrella and overcoat and heads off to the car park.

*****

St Mary's. 2 am. Just another piece of human frailty being wheel chaired in by paramedics. Unusually, this one's wearing a suit and a shirt and tie.

"What have we got?"

"Found him sleeping rough, under a hedge. Blood all over him, but no sign of injury."

Sam Caldwell puts his head back and screams. His eyes are open wide, staring sightlessly. If only he could find words to describe what he sees. The bonnet of his car. A pile of blood and feathers. A dead pigeon lies featherless on a broken wing mirror, its skin bearing the evidence of recent plucking. Its neck is stretched like over-used chewing gum. Its bulging eyes stare up at him, conveying an unspoken message.

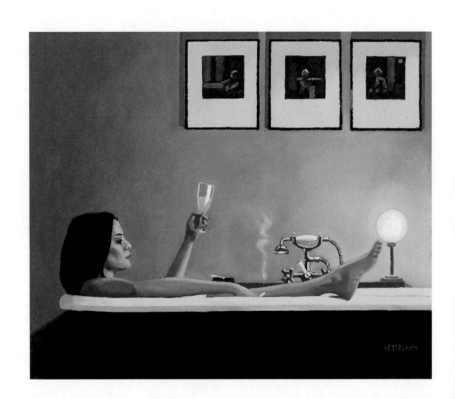

Night Time Rituals

Laura wobbled her way to the door and left the ward. Her colleagues sighed with relief. She was having a particularly bad day with her feet and was even more irritable than usual. It seemed that everyone knew about Laura's feet; they were as legendary as Florence Nightingale's lamp. Laura had Plantar Fasciitis.

Even when she was standing still, she rocked from side to side – like one of those porcelain dolls with badly moulded feet. She even took to wearing dolly shoes: dainty and flat but sensible enough to hold the inner soles which cost £200 but were worth every penny because you can't be too careful about looking after your feet. Every polite enquiry about her feet resulted in an obsessively detailed and meticulously delivered report: the initial consultation with the podiatrist (a very clever man – do you know there are over 300 bones in the foot?); the plaster of Paris moulds for the bespoke orthotics; the comfort of a hot bath followed by lashings of Ibuprofen gel.

Laura became her feet. Having spent over thirty years as a necessary appendage to her legs, they now became an extension of her psyche, her core, her inner being. Her feet determined what she had for lunch. On good days she hobbled to the canteen. When she'd overdone it they throbbed like she'd walked on hot coals and she ate student nurses in a corner of the ward. Laura's husband also suffered acutely from her feet. The pain was unbearable; worse than the very worst headache she'd ever had and *always* worse when she took her weight off them. Her feet moved to the top of the list, relegating all other maladies and indispositions to mere trifles.

Laura was one big pair of feet. She spat out the calluses and corns in venomous rages. Her toe nails grew longer and longer and poked her friends in the eye if they didn't enquire after the progress of their close companion. And as her feet grew more and more troublesome, they swallowed up her whole body and wobbled off to look for another.

Today had been a particularly bad day. The sweat was pouring out of them and every part of them ached and throbbed. They tried to be reasonable but what could they do when they were so abused. The others didn't have to put up with this. Every night when they went home they were able to chill out - kick off their shoes and rest awhile. They worked hard all day and expected a bit of time to themselves but it wasn't to be. They couldn't remember the last time they'd had a good soak in the bath - in fact, they couldn't remember much at all these days. This morning, they'd just leapt into the shower when they'd been called away to look at the kitchen calendar to check whether it was actually a work day or not. It was - so after being scalded for a few seconds because the shower still hadn't been mended, they'd had a minute or two's attention and then been squeezed into their shoes - ready for the onslaught. After plodding up and down the stairs five or six times, looking for car keys, they were finally ready to face another day.

As they made their way to work, they pondered on the meaning of life. Had they been able to make a difference? Had they done a good job? They'd served some purpose. Without feet, there would have been no Giant Leap for mankind; no-one would ever have been able to think on their feet; there'd be no Bigfoot in the North American Forests. They were obsessing again. Sometimes they thought they ruled the world.

They'd never wanted it to be like this. It wasn't as if they had much in common nowadays. Years ago, they'd been like two peas in a pod. Attractive - glamorous even - ready for anything. Now they were at odds not just with one another but with the whole world, or so it seemed. Not that long ago, they'd shuffled in intimate clinches on night club dance floors, then staggered home in anticipation of sliding between the sheets. They'd rocked and rolled and run naked on a beach in Italy. Their toes twitched with delight at the memory of the warm sand that got absolutely everywhere and they considered doing it all again, but corns and callouses screamed in indignation at the very idea and brought them back to earth with a jolt. Sure, they could still rock and roll but it wasn't the same. Although they were still young enough to know better, they rocked and rolled like old people lumbering painfully through the motions, trying to keep their balance. They still enjoyed an occasional walk on a sandy beach but there was no nakedness now, only sensible sandals and sometimes socks. Although by necessity they still shared the same space, the touching days were over. They kept their distance and reconciled themselves to the fact that they'd be together until the day they died. That was just the way it was. They were running away from the present, but not fast enough to return to the past and with the future creeping up on them like a festering sore. They had nowhere to go.

On better days, they dug in their heels and tried to recreate their youth. Some tender, loving care, a massage and a few loving words made all the difference. It didn't happen often, but it seemed that today might just be one of those days.

It had been one hell of a day for both of them. It had begun with a terse exchange.

"D'you think we're still suited?"

"I'm afraid I'm late. We'll talk tonight"

And they'd carried on being afraid all day. They were always afraid. Afraid that someone might step on their toes and cause them to spit like a trodden-on snake; afraid that they might step on somebody else's toes and earn the disapproval that would undermine their shaky confidence; afraid that they might wobble or fall down or let somebody else down. Life was one long fear: fear of getting old; fear of not being up to the job; fear of living; fear of dying. They couldn't bear suffering - their own or other people's.

Yet now they walked to the car with a lighter step and wallowed in the realization that they ached less than usual and actually fitted inside their shoes instead of spilling over the top like a couple of muffins. Their toes laughed and smirked and wriggled in anticipation of a long soak in a bubbly bath and even an early night. They knew that they had to face up to the inevitable. They knew that if they made an effort they could still dance to slower tunes with smaller steps. They were old enough to dance with their hearts as well as their legs; old enough to dance even if they looked like fools. And when they'd finished dancing, they would walk down to the fish and chip shop and have a cone of chips and a piece of battered cod and wash it down with a nice cup of tea. They'd run up the stairs to see which of them could get into bed first because the last one in has to turn out the light. And in the darkness one foot would rub against a leg and one leg would wind itself around another. The calluses and corns and venomous rages would simply melt away, as all pain does in heaven. And all would be well with the world.

Yes, it had indeed been one hell of a day but it had ended with a promise of heaven.

They were both were hungry for change, for something new and different.

Decisions were made: a smart pair of shoes - something a bit stylish; a candlelit dinner. It would do them good. They deserved it. Perhaps they could have a weekend away by the sea.- splash about in the rock pools like they had when they were younger; take in the sea air; feel the old tingle of excitement.. Ok, so they were older and less tolerant and it wasn't always easy to cope with the strains of the job. But they had nothing to fear. They were still alive and kicking and they had to make the most of it.

******

Laura almost fell through the front door. She kicked off her shoes and, leaning on the wall, flexed her feet in turn, wiggling her toes. Harry raised his eyebrows and handed her a glass of wine.

"You're spoiling me."

"And why not? Feet sore?"

"Not so bad darling. Nothing a good soak and a massage won't put right."

Laura poured took the wine and headed upstairs.

Harry waited for a few moments and then followed. The bathroom door was ajar and wafts of steam and rose-scented bath oil invited him into the bathroom. He peered inside and a glass of wine and a rather elegant leg was perfectly framed in the doorway. He pushed the door open and caught his breath. The condition of the foot and its partner might be questionable but the rest of Laura's body was as beautiful as it had ever been. She turned towards him and smiled.

He picked up the foot which was resting on the edge of the bath and massaged it gently.

"Mmm ..."

Laura closed her eyes and leaned back her head. Harry put his other hand in the water and stroked her leg.

Their night time rituals may never be the same again

Original Sin

There is no present or future, only the past, happening over and over again, now.
EUGENE O'NEILL, *A Moon for the Misbegotten*

3750 BC
Velvet darkness. Night gave rest to my weariness; wrapped me in death, just for a moment, until the dawn of welcome light gave shape to the hours and showed me the way to the water of life which cooled and sustained me.

All living creatures, birds, beasts and Adam and I were fed and comforted. He liked what he'd made. We two shared in his delight - and ate the good fruit

Depths of darkness – night. I hide, heart pounding, awake; afraid of death's cloak just for a moment, until the light of endless day shames my nakedness and shows me the way to the water of death which threatens to drown me. Now all living creatures, birds, beasts and see me through sore eyes.

We'd liked what he'd made so he'd shared in our delight, testing the strength and goodness of our hearts; wanting only perfection yet creating only sin.

And now my sons and their sons and their sons and daughters are blighted.

1960 AD
I knew that I still existed even though I had just seen the Angel of Death. He had stood at my head holding a drawn sword on the tip of which was a drop of bittterr gall. When I saw him, I had cried and the heavenly messenger had thrown the gall into my mouth. I wasn't afraid. I felt honoured and privileged to have been called. I had been preparing for this moment for a long time. Maybe a

hundred years, maybe just a second or two. The clock on the wall told me nothing and yet its presence was sinister. My heart had stopped beating but the clock gave an indefinable shape and rhythm to my being which I didn't understand. I only knew that I must not let it out of my sight until I was told to do so.

I felt that I could still see, and smell, and taste and touch and hear. This surprised me. Perhaps I was not dead after all. Like a butterfly I crawled out of the black dress I had been wearing and was glad to do so. I touched the face, blue and wrinkled, and recoiled as I smelt the sorrow that its wearer had endured. I hoped that this was the last time that I would ever smell sorrow but I had to smell it now. If I turned away she would have to smell it forever, in the place where sorrow lived in a black hole.

From the deepest and ugliest wrinkles of the face emerged seven hideous creatures, each beckoning me to climb back inside, to continue their bidding. I leaned over the face and let the sorrow of sin waft over me. The sorrow of the sin of lust enveloped me first, delivered by Asmodeus, the demon of lust responsible for twisting people's sexual desires. Asmodeus, now handsome and engaging, used his charms to compel me to look at the number 1 on the face of the clock. This I did, unknowingly aware that the clock's face was as telling as the face I'd left behind in my discarded body. This number was white, slight, the smallest of all the numbers. It was a baby boy. One month old and given away; an unwanted gift born of pain and heartache. I touched the whiteness of his muslin nappy and heard my own white, screaming wail as they took him away and left me empty.

My own wailing became that of Asmodeus as the clock struck one and the whiteness of the light revealed Raphael, Angel of God's healing force. Asmodeus shrank in horror as Raphael put the baby in my arms, followed by all the unwanted babies of the world.

I was assailed next by Mammon, the demon god of avarice and riches. The clock's number 2 leapt out and showed itself, elegant and curvaceous. Two was a haughty female, lounging on a coach, fondling a golden apple. The clock struck two. Raphael was not done yet. He seized the apple and, as he did, the demon Mammon launched himself at the angel and wrestled him. Strengthened by the clock's dazzling twoness, Raphael wrapped two hands, two wings and two legs around Mammon's neck and hurled him down to his earthly cave stacked high with worldly treasure. Whispering softly, Raphael shared with me the real riches of the prodigal son.

Beelzebub, Lord of the Flies, Chief Demon and renowned trouble-maker, sneered and filled the room with shiny red 3s before I even had chance to look at the clock. I wretched as the taste of heady red wine and the juice of fruit and meat evidenced my gluttony and fermented into fear in the pit of my belly. Again Raphael fought for me as the clock struck. It wasn't difficult to overcome Beelzebub, whom he reduced to a mere shadow of his fly-like self by swatting him three times and flicking him into a vat of shiny red blood shed by God's son to save the world.

I was still sure that the Angel of Death had returned to God without my soul, on account of my sinful ways. I was crying for my Lord, in anguish at his having deserted me. I knew that I had sinned but I couldn't believe he was rejecting me. The remaining demons taunted me in turn, in a desperate bid to persuade me to renounce my faith:

"Why did God make you?"

My spirit was still strong and I shouted out boldly:

"God made me to know Him, to love Him, and to serve Him in this world, and to be happy with Him forever in the next."

"No he didn't - he made you because he was bored and he needed something to do."

The demons cackled in unison and called up reinforcements from the other demons of the deadly sins to interrogate me. Lucifer, the fallen angel, arch enemy of God, charged me with pride and I almost drowned in the memories of my own Leviathan,

Demon of Envy and the chief gate-keeper of Hell painted me green and I smelt the envy and desire I'd felt as I'd longed for forbidden fruit. Then it was the turn of Amon, demon of wrath. He hurled himself at my fading spirit, butting me with his head and lashing me with his snake's tail. Breathing fire, he spat the ashes of the past and the sparks of the future and burnt my soul with the scorched crimson of my anger and intolerance. My beleaguered soul was spared the hostilities of Belphegor who had planned the final provocation on the subject of sloth. He just couldn't be bothered to turn up.

I was fighting for my life. I felt sure that my life on earth was not likely to continue and for that I was strangely grateful. I had no desire to re-enter the crumbling remains which lay beneath me and yet I felt strangely compelled to climb back into their familiarity. Battling with the urge to squeeze back in via any orifice which would allow me entry, I touched the mouth and tried to force it open.

As I did so, the lips took on a redder hue and were no longer parched and dry. Lascivious and eager, they were a lover's lips and it was VE day with vanloads of beer, spam sandwiches, urgent kisses and desultory sex with no thought of the consequences. Unseeing eyes in hollow cheeks flickered back to life and I peered into the past and re-lived the years in a kaleidoscope of time which did not actually exist. The space around me suffocated me and I gasped for air to drink and water to breathe. I tasted the sky of my childhood holidays, swam in the golden sea and swallowed sea-gull sandwiches. A gaudy deckchair howled with laughter as it trapped dad's fingers and mum's ice-cream cornet melted with delight as he threw his cigarette onto the li-lo and it popped like a fart at a vicar's tea-party.

Words of warning and cries of condemnation bombarded me but I chewed the words and spat them out into a bucket of coal and they put them on the fire. I chewed another million words and tried to swallow them but spewed them up into the snow, spoiling its perfection and leaving my mark, like a dog relieving its bursting bowel.

For now it was winter and my dad was digging us out of the back door and I waded through white clumps of vagueness until I reached the summer where my husband was waiting for me. I touched the lingering stench of my dying body and, as I did so, I felt no urge to climb back in. I knew that I had no use for it now. I had been drowning in the Sea of Life and Death but now I felt a clarity and purpose that held me in its arms and comforted me. I knew that I was free but that the battle was not yet over. I must keep up the fight. I knew that if the demons had their way I would burn in hell. Hell was a trap and the road to its gates was lined with hope. I knew that I would follow this road willingly, propelled by guilt and shame, for such is the nature of the human condition. It was all a matter of faith.

Desperate to find some relief from the power of the guilt which choked me, I sought the memory of the promise of forgiveness which had sustained me in my life on earth. Only that would enable me to turn her back on the demons. The nausea of my imperfections was overwhelming and bodily fluids seeped and leaked from every orifice of my earthly body as it fought to rid itself of its shame.

Raphael knew that his strength alone would not be sufficient to save me. He called on Michael, Prince of Light, on Uriel and Gabriel and all the cherubims and seraphims to unite in persuading me of God's forgiveness.

My spirit soared at the sight below and as the past transcended the present and became the future, I heard my lord calling from the depths of my despair: He cried out with a loud voice:

Lazarus, come out!

The dead man came out, his hands and feet bound in white strips and his face wrapped in a cloth. He guided me away from the path of shame and the demons howled in indignation.

I walked toward the bright light. I was filled with joy and a feeling of peace. But, unexpectedly, the nearer I got, the dimmer the light became and the joy and peace took on a menacing glow which frightened me. As the light died, I peered down at theme I'd left behind. I touched the face and smelt again the sorrow and the pain. I crawled back into the lifeless shell and its foulness overpowered me.

I opened my eyes and saw the clock on the wall. I looked around the room. Nothing out of the ordinary. I was back.

This was hell. Hell was the endurance of pain, relentless guilt and eternal shame. This was the black hole where sorrow lived forever.

Table for One

Brookhaven is a building quite separate from the rest of the hospital. It is an attractive, building with clean lines of symmetry, a sense of order and nothing to identify its purpose. Its inhabitants lack these qualities in abundance.

The nature of their condition is not modernised as easily as the building, in spite of the plethora of drugs and therapies which surround them. The tormented shout and scream but the devils remain; the depressed weep tears of despair and salt runs into their wounds but does not cleanse them.

The pencils are arranged in order of size; the pens according to colour; the notebooks alphabetically; half a dozen novels organised by thickness and height: Collins; Chandler; Keyes – all examples of good work in their own genre. Ellen shuffles them around; decides on chronological order. Everything is ready. Her little table in the corner. Just for her. Time to begin. Maybe a little something in the style of Jackie Collins. Something steamy for starters.

She takes her best pencil and writes:

She found herself a little table in the corner. A table for one. She looked around for Luigi – her usual waiter, what should she have to start? She glanced up at the 'Today's Specials' board. She might try the trout pate ...or maybe salmon mousse. She remembered the first time she ate trout. She bought it from the little market in Chioogia. She'd spent such happy mornings there during that long summer - twice a week Fridays and Tuesdays - and then on to that little restaurant for lunch. It's difficult to say which she enjoyed most for each had its own delights and titillated her various appetites. Marco, her favourite stall-holder, let her handle the slithering eels and salt cod before she made her choice. Marco understood her. He knew that the pungent smell and slippery touch of his wares was as satisfying as the eventual dish which she'd enjoy later - with a complement of white wine, a little oil and a large helping of authentic and inimitable Italian sauce. Marco's seafood was similarly appealing and, as they bartered, whispering excitedly behind their hands, she'd stroke her fingers longingly across hard shells which hid sweet delights, tiny shrimps not yet spoiled by the toughness of maturity and lobsters, red with rage - dominant, assertive, their claws tied up, interestingly, in rubber bands to stop them drawing blood.

She looked back at the menu. She felt faint and weak with hunger and anticipation. There was no sign of Luigi. She guessed it must be his day off. As always, the food on display bore little relation to the printed menu. You never really knew what you'd get. That's what made it so exciting. A waiter she'd never seen before made his way over to her table. She drooled at the thought of what was to come and touched his arm, smiling, asking what he'd suggest. He suggested she call him Toni. He told her that he'd look after he just like Luigi did; that Luigi had left special instructions that senorita should have the best of everything. His enthusiasm was infectious. He obviously had a penchant for strawberry blondes, just like Luigi did. It must be an Italian thing! His suggestions whetted her appetite even more, bringing such pleasure to him as well as to her. He was obviously passionate about his work. She ordered the pate, then waited patiently, folding and refolding the pure white table napkin, fingering the expensive cutlery, placing the dessert spoon neatly next to its matching fork. Perfect partners. Everything was ready. Just a matter of time. These things couldn't be rushed. Her stomach churned, saliva trickled down her throat and she licked her lips longingly. It finally arrived. The waiter smiled an exquisite smile as he placed it lovingly on the table. And she stared down at a wedge of putty garnished with tired salad and two triangles of curled up toast. Was nothing as it seemed?

She's bored. Her writing is salad tired and putty-ish. Stodge. She feels a touch of Raymond Chandler is needed. Something punchy, no-nonsense, 'hard-boiled'.

Was nothing as it seemed? There was a guy over at the round table in the corner. A table for one. He was on the goddamn phone. Eating, American style, with one hand. Scampi and chips. No big decisions. No finesse. Sounded like NYPD. She pushed the pate round the plate. What she heard next sure made her glad it wasn't chicken livers.

"Yeh, buddy, that's it. Down on Ainsworth's farm. When I first saw him, he was trussed up like a chicken in the corner of the coop. I'd have bet my bottom dollar that he'd been murdered by some hired hand on the farm until the girl pointed out that it was holiday and no-one was working. The girl was wailing like a banshee, tearing at his clothes and my ear drums, like this was the beginning of the end of her life – or the end of the beginning of something even bigger. It was obvious she knew the guy and even more obvious that he knew her. I caught sight of the photo lying beside him in the blood and guts. It was her. This was an open and shut case. I'd stake my life on it.

She just kept right on wailing: 'It's his birthday today! He had the day off special.' Green snot ran down her face like the candles on the cake he'd never see. She said his da had bought him a new set of wheels. She pointed to the nippy red sports car on the other side of the field. It was a sure bet that this dead chicken had made a mean living out of something or nothing.

She was a blonde – a strawberry blonde. A dizzy blonde. A strawberry milkshake. All froth and no milk."

She wishes Chandler would go away. She needs to get it down. It's her story. She can't lose her train of thought. But as Chandler disappears, her head empties. She knows the story but she doesn't know how to put it into words. She picks up her books and glances at a picture of Marion Keyes. She flicks through the first couple of pages and words tumble onto the paper.

"All froth and no milk. A bloody useless cappuccino! Nothing changes!" The owner of the voice got up from the glass table near the door – a table for one – and moved towards the bar to join a clone of herself. She handed the girl a glass of chilled wine and clambered onto a bar stool.

"Like the hair, Fiona. That shade of blonde really suits you darling. So how are you? What are you doing now, Fiona?" Insincerity oozed from her lips like pus from a teenage boil.

"I'm still at St Agatha's. Head of Drama." The girl extended her fingers, examined her immaculate nails and arched her back, leaning on the bar with the nonchalance of a recovering alcoholic.

Her friend smiled. "You would be Head of bloody drama. You've fulfilled your early promise, then. You were the biggest drama queen at St Peter's Comprehensive!"

"D'you remember the day you told Mrs Gee that Luigi Mancini had put his hand up your skirt and put a note in your knickers?"

The girl's gaze remained fixed on the fingernails. She stroked each one in turn, as though she were preparing them for some sort of action. The only clue to the fact that she'd heard what had been said was the slight bobbing of an Adam's apple as she appeared to quickly swallow a venomous response.

"I married him." The girl sniffed just slightly as she paired up the fingers of each hand into a steeple shape. "He works in this restaurant, as a matter of fact. His father owns it."

Her friend gulped, coughed and sprayed the girl with house white and splinters of peanut.

"For God's sake! Be careful! This coat cost a month's salary!"

"What? I can't believe you're that badly paid! Not a Head of Drama! Anyway, Fiona, get back to the bloody point! Does Luigi Mancini still put notes in your knickers? Or does he just tell you when he wants a quick grope?"

The girl's face crumpled. Her friend peered at her. Something wasn't quite right. The tears were real; the make-up slid off her face with alarming speed and revealed true distress - along with three spots and more lines than a map of Britain. Within just a few seconds the Head of Drama was a character in a major tragedy. But this time, it seemed for real. Her friend bit her lip. She reached over and squeezed the girl's hand. "Don't upset yourself, Fiona. Whatever is the matter?"

"I can't tell you." Fiona was beginning to sound more like her old self. She was overdoing the snivelling.

"Can't? Or won't?"

"You wouldn't understand."

"Of course I would. I'm a bloody psychologist, aren't I? That's what I do. I understand!"

"We're separated .... Luigi's a serial adulterer"

"What? And you still come in here?"

"Only on his days off ... it's his day off today. It's his birthday. His father always gives him the day off on his birthday. That - and some really lavish gift."

"Why did he go out looking for sex with other women? Or, in the words of Paul Newman..."

"Why go out for hamburger when you have steak at home?"

Fiona closed her eyes as though she were remembering. Suddenly, and without a word, she climbed down from the bar stool and fled from the restaurant.

The sound of brakes brought the place to a standstill. The loud American, the psychologist, the waiter - and every man and woman - stared into the street at the lifeless body as it was stretchered into an ambulance.

She gulps and bursts into tears, she knows that she just has to try to be herself if she's ever going to get over it. She can't be other people. She glances at the Collins, the Chandler, the Keyes. They can't make it go away. The writing's supposed to be helping her. Therapy. That's why she's here."

She's tired of Fiona and her psychologist friend. She's tired of Marco and his double-entendres and patronising waiters and tables for one and other people's conversations. She's tired. She, herself, writes steadily and slowly:

Her breasts rose and fell in a rhythmic desperation that gave them a life of their own. Heavy, desperate breaths punctuated the chaos in his mind. He couldn't go on for much longer and he began for the first time to consider the possibility that he wasn't cut out for this – that there was something missing from his technique, his experience. This had happened so many times before. He carried on, sweating and trembling and the veins in his forearms bulged and throbbed under his body weight. His heart pounded as *he looked at the blonde hair spread out across the bed; pearls of perspiration dripped onto her face and, in a moment of fanciful relief, he thought they could be tears – perhaps of joy or expectation. He wanted her to open her eyes, to look at him, to understand that the man pounding away was not the same man as the sadistic stranger who'd raped her in the dark shadows of his alcoholic world and then pushed her into the path of a passing car. He wanted her to know that her husband was in the hospital waiting room, waiting. Waiting for his wife to return from the dead so that they could carry on living and loving.*

He knew he'd have to stop. Voices in his head told him to call it a day, that it was no use.

"OK. Is everyone agreed? Time of death: 2.32."

She puts down her head onto her little desk and sobs. If only she knew whether she was alive or dead.

The Drifter

Alan bit into the bacon sandwich and the sandwich bit back. It screamed in indignation at his hypocrisy and he just had to agree. Inevitably, the rumbles in his stomach screamed louder and he savoured the greasy slices of pig with guilt flavoured relish.

"For God's sake, Alan! Why are you eating bacon sandwiches at this hour of the night? It's totally inappropriate! It's two o'clock in the morning! You've woken me up! The bloody house is full of smoke and smother!"

He rolled his eyes and, raising two greasy fingers upwards in a gesture of defiance, put the unwashed grill pan into the sink, lit a cigarette and poured another large whisky.

In the early days of his marriage, he'd been enjoying a sandwich like this when his wife had told him that she didn't know how he could eat dead flesh when he spent so much time dissecting it. He'd been foolish enough to be deliver a lecture about the differences between surgery and butchery, uncompromising in its graphic detail. Suzie had demanded to know how he knew so much about it and he'd drawn into the memory of one of the pleasures of his childhood on his grandfather's farm.

Autumn was butchering time, a period of joy in the harvest of the year's work and of sadness that the lives of your beautiful, healthy animals had come to an end. On this occasion the animals had to be treated with the same kindness and respect with which they were treated during their lives. Good farmers raise their animals free from fear, anxiety and stress. The animals should meet their end as they lived, without the terror of the slaughterhouse. Alan sighed and pondered the inevitable analogy.

Last night had been difficult. The last thing he'd expected to find when he'd opened the old lady up was a gangrenous bowel. There was too much of it to re-section – if she'd survived the surgery, her quality of life would have been appalling. She was a feisty old bird – he owed her more than that. Her daughter seemed to have taken it quite well. It hadn't been an easy conversation. It never was in these circumstances. She'd known something was wrong when he approached her in his scrubs.

She'd been full of questions. He wasn't going to lie to her, but even if he'd tried her eyes would have extracted the answers from his.

She'd died under the anaesthetic, hadn't she? No. He'd left her alive on the operating table but they'd found a huge clot in an artery in her abdomen; most of her gut was, to all intents and purposes, dead.

He'd taken the girl's hand and said "It's a bit like having a heart attack in your tummy."

She'd bridled, snatched her hand away and wanted to know the proper medical terminology.

"Mesenteric infarction."

He'd explained that he could remove the dead gut but that her quality of life would be appalling. She'd wanted to know what the alternative was. He'd told her. She'd looked him squarely in the eye:

He'd smiled a long, lingering smile. He found her attractive and felt an inappropriate disappointment that she'd snatched away her hand.

'Inappropriate' was a word that Suzie had used a great deal recently. It was inappropriate that people over fifty still talked about sex; inappropriate that anyone should hold hands in public; inappropriate that he should walk round their bedroom naked. Anybody could walk in – even, apparently when the house was empty of all but its inhabitants.

Alan smiled and picked up the *Telegraph*. He supposed it was inappropriate that he'd not finished the crossword on his way home this evening. He usually did. He was a creature of habit. Clues down in the morning; clues across in the evening. This morning, though, his attention had been distracted by a leggy blonde. That led to him not completing the morning clues. No wonder the day had gone badly. How could he answer questions about life and death when he hadn't even read today's cryptic clues. He shivered and switched on the fan heater in the corner of the kitchen.

He stared at 4 across:

Tube taken to theatre for three-act play (8)

Bloody hell! There was no escape! Even the crossword was taking the piss! He laughed out loud. His pen stabbed at the paper as he inserted the answer – CATHETER. He threw down the paper and closed his eyes.

He could still see this morning's leggy blonde. Stunning.

"D'you think we'll be delayed for long?"

Alan had looked up at the girl who was jammed in the aisle, standing beside him. He realized that the train had come to a halt.

"Sorry. Sorry to disturb you. It's just that I'm worried about being late."

"Don't be sorry - and no, I don't think the delay will be too long. We have this nearly every day."

His eyes left her face and travelled down her body to a pair of magnificent legs. Clearly, this young lady's constituent parts were not in need of any attention other than an appreciative glance. Furthermore, he could now confirm that his own body parts seemed to be in good working order!

The matter of the efficiency of his sexual organ had rather preoccupied him lately. He knew that Suzie was losing patience with his fumbling attempts. Her irritation was ill-concealed just as his indifference towards her was increasing day by day. He knew they were drifting apart.

"It's the amount of bloody whisky you're drinking Alan. It's got nothing to do with your age - for God's sake, you're only 55."

He knew he was staring at the girl. He couldn't avoid it. She looked really nervous – anxious even.

"What're you late for?"

"New job. At the hospital. Got to be there for ten."

"You'll be cutting it fine, but you should just about make it."

Alan tried to smile reassuringly but decided that it must have been the smirk of a middle-aged lecher because the girl looked away and stared hard at an advert for M&S. She didn't look like an M&S girl – more *Next*, he'd say. His wife was M&S, as the monthly bill confirmed! He couldn't understand how one woman could wear so many clothes. She must wear them in layers, like an onion, or it would take several years to get through everything in her wardrobe. Not that he knew much about her clothing – outerwear or underwear. Clothes were peeled off in the dark and stuck back on in the bathroom. She came straight out of one of those cardboard doll books. You cut out the dolls and the dolls' clothes and then dressed and undressed them. His sister had them when she was a child. He could remember the dolls faces so clearly, with their bright red lips and artificial smiles that never changed. He used to wonder what his sister could see in something so lifeless. He'd decided it must be a 'girl thing'. Now he knew it wasn't.

He poured another whisky and agreed with his dick that the long-legged blonde had been a good start to the day. The bodies he'd subsequently encountered had been less attractive. After lunch, he'd done his ward rounds and endured another two hours of poking flabby abdomens and recalcitrant bowels and peering into yawning rectal cavities which belied the theory that God created man in his own image and likeness.

He smiled at the blasphemy of this and assured himself that non-believers wouldn't be damned for such thoughts. The smile left his face as he considered that if he were truly a non-believer, the idea of being 'damned' would hold no concerns. His brow furrowed. Death was as complicated as life. He swirled the whisky round the glass. It was the colour of deep brown piss. The piss of jaundice. His mind was awash with the piss and shit of thirty years of medicine. He wished he could have saved the old woman.

Failure! Alan closed his eyes and considered the fragility of life and all its constituent parts. He supposed he'd drifted into medicine because he wanted to make a difference but not even the combined power of his medical expertise and the miracles of the pharmaceutical industry could save them all. Only God could do that!

Good God! Good, good God! This non-existent being seemed to be dominating his sodden brain tonight. He blamed the old woman's daughter for that. She'd brought up the subject and now the whisky was pickling the idea in his head, presumably in an attempt to preserve it for future use. Well, it needn't think it was going to be a permanent feature.

The daughter had been upset at his suggestion about her mother's treatment.

"You can't expect me to make a decision like that. I don't play God. What would you do if she were your mother?"

"She's not."

"If she were."

He'd shaken his head, staring at her. He wondered who'd blink first. She did.

"No way I'd want her to live like that. I'd just want her to drift away."

Alan obviously thought he was God. If so, he'd got a lot l to answer for.

He'd actually got a great deal to answer for, even if he wasn't God. He couldn't win really. If he was God, he'd pre-destined that Suzie should have that stupid affair with his best friend. If he was God, why hadn't he forgiven her instead of trying to pay her back – tit for tit!! He smiled at his inebriate wit, staring into the crystal of the half-empty glass, cursing that it showed only the past and not the future. The glass was always half bloody empty. If he wasn't God, he'd demonstrated startling arrogance in expecting her to live by his rules because of one mistake. If he wasn't God, why had he decided that the old woman would be better off dead?

Alan sloshed more scotch into the glass and took a deep gulp. The more he drank, the more the glass was half-full. It swam before his eyes and the amber liquid was no longer piss but the wine of the wedding feast at Cana. Maybe the woman was better off dead, and he, in God-role, had made an excellent decision. When he'd last seen her, she certainly seemed to be enjoying the prospect of her journey into the unknown. The chaplain was with her. The mumbo-jumbo of religious rites wasn't new to him. He'd witnessed these spectacles and rituals many times. They usually annoyed him. Over the years, he'd got more than a little hacked off with God's interference in his daily work. If they pulled through, it was *Thanks be to God*; if they didn't make it, it was because the NHS was fucked up.

Today had been different though. He'd felt compelled to stay in the room until the words were finished. He knew the old woman was almost gone, but her face had exuded a serenity that permeated his cynicism and sent a shiver through the bones of all the dead he'd failed to save. He felt their presence and they forgave him his trespasses but demanded that he forgive those who'd trespassed against him. And the bones of the living strengthened him in an earnest desire to sin no more and to be delivered from evil.

Alan poured the contents of the glass down the sink. Now it was neither half-empty nor half-full. He stared into the faceted crystal and the future was clearer than it had ever been.

He picked up the suitcase he'd packed a couple of weeks ago.

On the Border

"Shall we have a take-away if I'm going to be late? I can pick up a Chinese and text you when I'm on my way back."

He picked non-existent hair and bits of fluff from his Italian suit. "Shall we?"

The duvet grunted some sort of reply. He glanced at the shapeless figure which now occupied the centre of the bed. He sighed.

The duvet grunted again.

"Whatever!"

He tutted, ran down stairs, picked up his briefcase and headed for the front door. He was about to close it behind him when the duvet grunted particularly loudly. No. Not loudly. Belligerently.

"Why do you have to go to Coventry today? We're going on holiday tomorrow. There's packing to be done. That takes forever."

The grunt had vacated the duvet and was on the verge of a temper tantrum. He knew the signs. He sighed, put down his briefcase and headed back up the stairs. Two at a time.

"Don't be silly darling. You know I've got to go. This meeting is very important.

"Piss off. It didn't have to be today."

"Oh, come on ..."

He looked at this watch. It was time he hit the road.

"Piss off .... piss off ...... piss off!"

The motorway. A grey blur of mist shrouded shapes hurtling their way towards the great metropolis. Each with its own cargo to be deposited in a place of its choosing for a purpose. To work. To play. To say hello or goodbye. To laugh or cry. To howl at some perceived wrong. To smile at a kindness. To touch a wrinkled hand or to stroke the soft head of a newborn. Journeys. Regular journeys; life-changing journeys.

All He wanted was to live a life where he could be himself. He never understood people very well anyway, and they never seemed to understand him either. All he wanted was his own world, his own reality. He wanted the open road to journey's end.

He found the house without difficulty. Mrs Greaves had already arrived and was in her car on the small drive. He squeezed in behind her. She got out and greeted him with a handshake that had the warmth and sincerity of a rattle snake which in this reincarnation was an estate agent.

"Aah. Good morning. So good to see you. Was your journey good?"

"Yes thank you."

He had no intention of making small talk with the woman. He was here to look around a house not on a blind date.

"Er. Goodo. How far are we from Kendal here in the sunny Midlands?"

"About 150 miles"

"Wife not with you then?"

He resisted the temptation to tell her that she was tied up in the boot of his car.

"No. She couldn't make it today."

The rattle snake put her eyes back into her head and opened the front door.

"Well here it is then. A nice house. Just needs a bit of TLC. Shall we start upstairs?"

The stair carpet was dated but clean. The sort they used to have in pubs, hotels and Indian restaurants. Black swirls with large red flowers hiding behind the pattern. Typically English. Expensive, but hard wearing and resistant to mud on shoes, red wine, vomit and Biryani. He remembered his mother and father buying carpet like this in the sixties.

The Rattle Snake opened a bedroom door.

"This is the master."

She stood back as he entered the room. He did a double take as he saw the double bed made up with a candlewick bedspread and the dressing table cluttered with the ephemera of older ladies.

"Why is the house still furnished?"

"Sudden death. The sale is in the hands of a solicitor. The contents will be removed after the house is sold."

He picked up one of the perfume bottles on the dressing table. *Blue Grass*. Old ladies' perfume. He closed his eyes and his mother wafted past him in her twin set and pearls. Sunday morning. On her way to church to pray for salvation of the world, for the sin and imperfection of the known and the unknown, that they might repent and see the glory of God.

Mrs Greaves broke into his thoughts. He sniffed the air as she spoke. Tobacco smoke and last night's garlic drifted on the end of the last notes of *Blue Grass* and the memory of his mother faded as they continued their tour of the upper rooms of the house.

They went first into a small bedroom complete with single bed occupied by a huge teddy bear. The walls were adorned with a motley collection - several posters including a 'Maggie Thatcher, Milk Snatcher' and a picture of John and Yoko. Above Teddy's head was a framed tapestry in which the words *Cry out To Jesus* had been stitched with care.

The spare room was a time warp of children's toys and books. Every bit of available space was occupied by years and years of Christmases, birthdays, and parental indulgences. He smiled at the pile of Enid Blyton and Arthur Ransome. The tottering piles of Matchbox toys still in their original boxes. Beano Annuals. Yoyos.

It's a mixed up world. The age of cowboys and spacemen: Davy Crockett and Roy Rogers lead the pack of western heroes that share the toy aisles with the out-of-this-world likes of Commando Cody and Tom Corbett competing with hula hoops and Frisbees, Fisher Price garages and Lego. He is with his mother, queuing on the stairs of Lewis's department store, waiting to see Santa and get his present. His mother's hand is warm and comforting and he enjoys this annual outing as much as the toy he gets from Santa. The man in the red cloak with sparkling eyes pulls her onto his lap and speaks kindly. He wishes his father was as kind as Santa.

"What's your name little boy?"

He feels a warm, fuzzy feeling inside as the eyes look into his and the cloak asks him what he'd like for Christmas.

He purses his lips. He wanted to sick to the business in hand.

"I'd like a yellow Porsche please."

Santa's bushy eyebrows shoot up.

"Well, Little Boy With No Name. Santa hasn't got one of those but I'm sure that my little helper will find you something nice in the grotto."

Santa's Little Helper is a dubious looking fairy in a ridiculous dress. She mooches around among the parcels and finds one with a blue label.

"How old are you little boy?"

He clucks with indignation but tells her that he's nearly six.

"This will do nicely for you."

He opens the tissue wrapped parcel with excitement and expectation. He hands the content to his mother and tears fill his eyes.

"Don't cry, sweetheart. I'll keep it for you. You might want it later"

She just about manages to get the green plastic mini into her coat pocket.

Mrs Greaves' rattle interrupts his thoughts.

"Time's getting on. I have another client at 2.30 pm. Let's make our way downstairs."

He sauntered behind the Rattle Snake as she led him to the lounge. Another pub carpet. The lounge had its own bar featuring Dubonnet, Advocaat, Cherry B and Babycham - for the ladies presumably - and Johnny Walker and Gordon's Gin for the men folk. He thought about the number of people who must have done the conga around this room, after unwrapping Christmas gifts of socks, slippers, handkerchiefs, talcum powder and other ill-chosen but well intentioned gifts bought from limited budgets and given with love and sincerity.

The kitchen was the last room to be 'viewed'. It was just a kitchen. A cooker. A fridge. No fancy gadgets. Just the basics required to produce a steak and kidney pudding or a beef stew. He caught sight of the old fashioned toaster – the sort where the two sides drop down – and remembered the one they'd had that caused his father so much anger. It was hard to believe that a grown man could lose his temper about burnt toast. His words rang in He's ears.

"For God's sake boy! Don't walk away and leave it. It only takes two or three minutes to do toast."

And He's mother would smile at him and whisper in his ear:

"I've put chocolate in your lunch box son. Your favourite."

She would squeeze his hand.

Hurry now. You'll miss the bus and get a late mark."

Mrs Greaves was clearly getting hot and bothered about her next client. She hurried her client towards the door.

"Anything you'd like to ask?"

"No thank you. I'll be in touch"

"It's a good house for the price. And it's vacant possession. No chain"

He nodded.

The journey home was slow. Now the traffic was crawling sloth-like. The greyness was no longer a blur, the shapes no longer shrouded in mist. Audis, Peugeots, Fords queued in the rush hour. He looked at the drivers. They looked tired, harassed, depressed, anxious. Whatever the reason had been for their journeys, few of them looked as though they had benefitted from them.

His mind drifted. He thought about the occupants of the house. He wondered how they'd lived, how they'd died, how they'd spent their years after the Dubonnet ran out.

He remembered the last time he'd seen his own parents. Their Silver Wedding Anniversary. They'd had a nice enough time. Went out for a family lunch at *The Navigation*. The afternoon was spent being interrogated by relatives he hadn't seen since his Granny's funeral and drinking cups of tea.

"What are you doing now?"

"Have you got your own house?"

"When are you settling down?"

He felt as though he were in a Game Show and if he answered all the questions correctly he would win a yacht or a 26 inch television.

That gave him an idea for a quick get-away.

"Sorry Mum. Got to go. Doing a pub quiz tonight for charity."

"You didn't say."

"Must have forgotten."

He picked up his car keys and kissed his mother.

"Aren't you going to say 'Goodbye' to the others?"

"Not much time. I'll see them soon enough. I suppose we're due another family funeral."

He smiled and his mother winced.

"I've made you some sandwiches for the journey son. And there's some chocolate. It's your favourite" She whispered conspiratorially and hugged him.

He'd known then that he could never see them again. He could make no contact – not even to explain why. The die was cast.

He was glad to get home and relax. To be in his own environment.

He put his key in the door and the love of his life bounded down the stairs.

They hugged and laughed.

"You've thrown off the duvet, then, and stopped sulking!"

"Of course. It won't take us long to get packed. How did your day go?"

"It was interesting. Quite a lot achieved."

He didn't need to tell him anymore than that. He'd never understand why he had felt he had to go back one last time.